Bequeathed a
Cutterville, Mississippi, Carol felt nothing but
grief.

"Grandpa, what will I do with your old
mansion and yesterday's ghosts?"

A week later, house closed, suitcases
packed:
"Look out Cutterville – I'm on my way!"

With the top down on her Corvette, a feeling of euphoria swept over her. Hair blowing wildly in the breeze, Carol looked around and saw that everything was the same, nothing had changed. She drove past the high school and on into town and parked next to the curb near the barber-shop, glanced about and sweet memories crept into her thoughts: At age sixteen the candy shop and the drug store on the corner had been important; Paul would buy her a sandwich and soda and hold her hand. She could still feel the sensation, the awakening and desire of young love. Where was he now? Had he followed his dream and become a lawyer? Had he married and left Cutterville? If she were to see him today would she still have that old feeling?

She got out of the car and headed down the street toward the candy shop. A bag of gum drops would be her dessert for the evening. Her luggage had been left in her grandfather's old mansion. A sandwich from the drug store, a coke and the gum drops would be tonight's dinner. Heels clicking on the sidewalk, she passed the barber-shop.

"Did you see that?" Paul asked, as he pulled the barber's cape off and went to the window. "Boy, I've never seen anything like that in this town."

Two other men and the barber followed him to the window. "I wonder where she came from and what she's doing here?"

"Well, I don't know," one replied, "but

whoever she is, I hope she stays!"

Paul paid Sam, the barber, and quickly left in order to follow the stranger down the street. His pulse quickened, something about the way she walked looked very familiar. Was it possible? At the corner she went into the candy shop and he sauntered in and stood beside her as she looked things over. Feeling him standing next to her, without turning, she said, "Please, go ahead and get whatever you like. It will take me awhile to decide."

The girl behind the counter smiled. "For goodness sake Paul, it's been a long time since you've been in. What can I interest you in?"

"A box of chocolates for my mother. You know the kind she likes don't you Shirley?"

"Yes, I do. What's the occasion? Is it her birthday or something?"

"No, I just thought it would be a nice surprise." He turned to the stranger. "I don't believe I've seen you here before," he stopped and caught his breath, "Carol! Am I dreaming? Is it really you?"

She laughed, "You finally noticed. Am I that easy to forget?"

"Forget? I never forgot you! You forgot me!"

Amused, Shirley said, "I take it you two must know each other."

"Know each other," he exclaimed, "I've been in love with her all my life!" He studied Carol's face. "I thought I had lost you forever, especially after your grandfather died. He was the last of the Nelsons in town." Forgetting about Shirley, he reached for Carol, "I think this deserves a hug. I hope you don't mind."

"Mind? Not at all, I've been waiting a very long time for this."

He embraced her and then held her at arms length, "I can hardly believe my eyes. What has happened to the freckles and where are your glasses? You have changed!"

Her arms slipped around his neck, "Yes Paul, I'm all grown up, lost the freckles and the glasses have been replaced with contacts." She backed away slowly and eyed him. He was a man and more handsome than in his youth. "You look the same, a little older but much more handsome than you were at age nineteen! I had no trouble recognizing you, even with all your muscles! I'm surprised you didn't know me!"

"Carol, you are so different, dignified and fashionable and citified, nothing like my high school sweetheart, except for the walk. You still have that follow me walk. It has been too long. No letters, nothing, and now all of a sudden you are here. Tell me you came back for me."

"Buy me a cup of coffee and I'll fill you in on everything. We have a few years to catch up with, a few lost years! Lost because you stopped writing."

"Just let me pay Shirley and we'll head across the street to Jim's coffee shop. Were you getting something?"

"Yes, I'll take a bag of gumdrops."

"Just add that to my bill Shirley," he said

and ushered Carol out and across the street.

Shirley, who had envisioned herself going with Paul, took the money, shook her head and gazed after them. "Can you beat that? Guess that rules me out."

Paul ventured a glance toward the barber shop and saw three faces watching through the front window. "You've caused quite a stir Carol. When I saw you walk by the barber shop I made a remark about the stranger who had just passed by the window. Now don't look, they are all there watching us. I know they are just busting to know who you are!"

"Won't they be surprised! I bet I went to school with all of them." They found a table and she ordered. "I've had nothing since I arrived so I'll have a sandwich and coffee. I had planned to swing by the grocery store and pick up a few things before going out to the house."

He ordered the same and reached for her hands, "The house? I don't think I'm following."

The sensation of his touch was the same as it had been in her youth. She pulled her hands away, "I came here hoping to learn what brought about my grandfather's demise. He left his old place to me and I will be occupying it for awhile. His death was very unexpected and came as a shock. Through the years we have kept in touch and he has always sounded as if he was in good spirits and feeling well. The news of his sudden demise saddens me. I loved him and grandma very much!"

Mentally picturing her alone in Nelson's

old mansion, he replied, "I don't know about you staying in that old house Carol. Maybe you should give it a little more thought. It has been empty ever since he died and is probably full of spiders and God knows what all. I doubt if it has electricity, running water or heat."

"I'm way ahead of you. I did a few things before coming; the lights have been turned on and the phone connected. I'm surprised Millie, at the phone company, has not spread the word. When I arrived I went directly to the house and left my luggage and you are right, it is a creepy mess! I am hoping to hire someone to help me clean and get it into shape. Nevertheless, I doubt it will hurt me to spend a few nights there while waiting. It will give me time to acquaint myself with things."

"Yes, I'm sure you would be fine, but I wish you had called me first. Consider this - stay with my mother and me until you have had some work done on it? You should be sure everything is functional before trying to move in and mom would love to have you! She often talks about your mother and father. She was very close to them. Also, through the years she has asked if I ever hear from you and you know the answer to that."

"Paul, how was I to know you were still here? Needless to say your offer is tempting and maybe I should take you up on it. That is, if you are sure it will not be an inconvenience. Your mother may object! She hasn't seen me in years and may not like the person I am now."

"There is nothing she would like better. She knew ours was a young love and after you left she saw my suffering. She will welcome you with open arms."

"I hope you're right because I would love to stay with you. First, however, I must go to the house and get my luggage. I can't live in the clothes I'm wearing."

"Deal! After we've had lunch I can drive you over to see mom and then take you out to your grandfather's place. How did you get here? Did you come by air, bus, train or drive?"

"I drove and you do not need to take me. I'll just go out, pick up my things and meet you back at your place. In the meantime you can warn your mother. Most women do not like unexpected guests. Are you married? If you are this might not be such a good idea."

"No, I am not married. No one could take your place. I live with mother. Since dad died, she needs me. Are you married?"

"No, I am not and have not given it a thought. I don't mean to mislead you. I've dated but not once have I been inclined to marry. Guess I kept waiting for that letter from you. The one that should have said, I need you."

"And I kept waiting for the same thing. The one that would say, come and get me. What was wrong with us? What were we afraid of?"

"We were young and you were heading off to college. My parents moved and we were separated. Being apart did not bring us closer. I had to be with them and you had to become a lawyer. I never forgot you and I never wanted anyone else. I've had offers but you have always been there in the back of my mind."

"And now here we are. Maybe there's a chance for us after all. We've lost allot of time, but we still have years ahead of us."

"Perhaps," she said, and stopped in front of a red convertible. "This is my car."

He grinned, "I should have known. I bet you get all kinds of attention in this thing!"

"Yes, I do and it makes me feel important. It's not a new car, I bought it second hand. It's in good shape and it makes me feel rich!" Wishing he would go with her she got in, started the engine and touched his hand, "Come with me."

He leaned over and gave her a kiss, "I could but should not, I have an appointment waiting for me at the office."

"Well," she sighed, "try to leave work early and I'll see you at your mother's house." She waved and drove off wishing she could stay with him.

How many nights had she lain awake thinking of him, wondering if he had married. Why had they drifted apart? Was it because they were young? Had he really longed for her the way she had longed for him? No matter, her feelings for him had never changed and if his actions were real he still loved her.

She stopped in front of the wrought-iron gates and looked up at the house:

Built in the year 1804, the thee-story

shingle style mansion still stood with dignity, pride and gentle aloofness amidst a grove of trees. Complete with two double wide chimneys on either side of the roof, verandas, walk round porches and two small windows near the top, it echoed with memories of the past. Despite its appearance she soon learned it needed attention; the steps leading up to the porch creaked and the door hinges squeaked.

Easing her way in, she shivered, turned on the lights and went upstairs to the bedroom where she had left her luggage. Considering the house had been closed for a long period of time the rooms were in very good condition, except for the dust and must. A quick look around and she closed the suit case she'd left opened on the bed and turned to leave but stopped to listen. Had she heard something?

"Hello, is someone here? If someone is here, I'll be right down." Receiving no response, she mumbled to herself, "This place is haunted! All old houses are haunted and these walls are trying to tell me something. Glad Paul asked me to stay with them. It's a little too soon for me to deal with granddaddy's ghost. This house will tell me all, in time."

Hurrying down the stairs she stepped out into the fresh air and locked the door. One last glance toward the roof and she fixed her eyes on one of the windows. Was someone there?

"My imagination," she said. Nevertheless, just in case, she smiled and waved, "I'll be back!"

The willow tree near the corner bent and whispered in the breeze. Her step hastened and she got into her car. Without looking back, she drove to the end of the drive, paused to close the gate and turned toward town.

As she recalled, Paul's house was an ordinary well kept cottage complete with picked fence, she parked in front and found Melba, Paul's mother, waiting at the door to greet her. "I'm so excited," she said, "I saw you park and wanted to be right here to give you a big welcome home hug. Paul said you had changed so much he didn't recognize you, but to me you look the same. I'm so glad he ran into you and asked you to stay with us. That spooky old house is not where you need to be. You should stay with us until you have taken care of business, made all your decisions and pulled everything together. What you need to do is sell that old place!"

Carol laughed and replied, "You haven't changed, still giving the orders and solving the problems. You always did boss me around, even when I was in high school. I remember it all, my dresses were to tight and my blouses too decolletage'. What do you think of me now?"

"You are as pretty as a picture, just like your mother and your grandma. They were both beauties. I hated to see you all move away. Your mother was like a sister to me and I missed her so much! Seeing you is like seeing her again. Now come on in and I'll show you to your room.

Our place is not as big as that old house but it has plenty of room for friends and relatives. Make yourself right at home. The drawers are all empty and so is the closet. The bathroom is a connecting one, but the room on the other side is empty. Paul's room is on down the hall next to mine. I like having him near me; it makes me feel safe. Just come out to the kitchen when you are ready. It will be awhile before Paul arrives. He had a client to see. He's a lawyer you know and has another divorce case to take care of. He hates divorce cases, doesn't like to see people separate." She smiled, "Now don't take too long! I'm anxious for our little talk."

"I'll be as quick as possible." As the door closed behind her Carol placed a suitcase on the bed, took out a few things, put them in drawers and hung the rest in the closet. Paul was right, before having to make decisions about her newly inherited estate, a night or so with them would give her a chance to pull her thoughts together. After a quick shower, she changed into a sweat suit and headed for the kitchen.

"I bet you're hungry aren't you? We'll eat as soon as Paul arrives. I'm sure he'll try to come home early. I'll start cooking as soon as he puts his foot through that door. How does some good old country fried chicken, mashed potatoes and gravy and all the fixings sound to you? This morning I baked a deep-dish blackberry pie. It's one of his favorites and he picked the berries. Bet you haven't had a homemade pie since you left!"

"Sounds like I'm home Melba. I haven't

had a good piece of friend chicken in years, and can't remember when I last had a piece of wild blackberry pie. I can hardly wait! How about a cup of coffee while we are waiting? Meanwhile, you can fill me in on a few things about my grandfather and grandmother. I am completely in the dark about his death."

Melba got their coffee, sat down and began to talk. "I just don't know where to start. Your grandfather's death is kind of a mystery to all of us. No one expected him to last long after your grandmother passed as they were so close. He was alone and depressed and for awhile it looked like he might grieve himself to death. Then, about a year later he came out of it and was his old self. He changed so much it was amazing! He was always a happy sort you know, laughing and joking! Most everyday you could find him in the barber-shop with the men talking politics and what's wrong with the world and such. He wasn't young but seemed to be in very good health and got along well with Gertie, the black lady who took care of his place, cooked for him and did his laundry and things. She had been with them for years.

He stayed in the upstairs bedroom as long as he could but one day he told Gertie to move his things into one of the rooms downstairs as he was finding it too hard to get up and down. I suppose she was happy to do it because Gertie is not exactly young. At any rate, he spent most of his time in his study and in the kitchen. So she moved all of his things, plus the pictures of your grandma down to one of the rooms that were for the servants, close to the kitchen. Gertie loved your grandaddy. Then one day she went over there to get him up and get his breakfast and found him dead.

There was no obvious reason for him to have died, seemed like his heart just stopped. They called it death by natural causes, but to tell you the truth honey he was so healthy I find it difficult to believe he just upped and died. Doc was even surprised and he had been taking care of him for years."

"Melba, what are you saying? Surely you don't think someone did him in? I can't believe that. For what reason? He had no enemies!"

"Well now don't let Paul know I told you this, but yes, I do! Everyone always said he had lots of money and maybe he did! I don't know! And there are those who think it is hidden in his house. I don't think he was the kind of man to hide money around his house. He was a very intelligent man. Yet, I suppose it is possible and there might be other things of value in the place, like antique jewelry and such. Your grandma had lots of that. He could have buried it."

"Your imagination is running rampant Melba and you are giving me the creeps. When I went out to pick up my suit case I could feel the presence of someone or something in the house. I called out but no one answered. Old houses spook me and I believe in the unseen. I'm surely glad Paul saw me and invited me to stay here with you for awhile because I don't think I could have slept there tonight. I'll have to get in touch with Gertie and see if she will help me get it cleaned up. I can't very well sell it the way it is, and I am not really sure that's what I want to do. Going through their old clothing and things is not something I look forward to. Nevertheless, it was left to me and I am the one who must get it done. I had no idea what I might be walking into and before coming here I gave myself a little pep talk. There is a question in my mind as to why he left it to me instead of Chad, his grandson. After all, Chad's father was in business with him."

Melba laughed, "You are just like your mother. She was a clairvoyant and knew things before they happened. If Gertie finds out about your special insight she will think you are a witch. I wish you luck! She is from the old school and believes in voodoo. Since she is the one who found your grandfather lying there dead, she is afraid to walk by or go near the old mansion. She is very superstitious and, when for some reason she must pass the old place at night, she swears she sees lights and ghosts in the upstairs rooms. Others have said the same."

"Oh, I didn't think about that! I suppose at night it is ghostly. But think of all the years she worked there without fear. Now, because of my grandfather's death, she is afraid. Does she still live in the same place?"

"Yes! My word she has a son and grand-children. Now here's a thought, one of her granddaughters does house work and she might be the one for you to ask!"

"Good idea! I'll ride out and visit with her tomorrow and ask if she or her granddaughter will help me with the place. She won't know who I am because she has not seen me in years. I'll have to ask if she remembers Edna Jane and James Nelson and tell her that I am their daughter."

The door opened and Paul entered, "Hey ladies, what's going on? Looks like mom has been filling you in on everything. She likes to talk! I bet she has been handing you all her superstitions and opinions about everything."

Carol laughed, "Well don't be surprised to hear I have a few of my own. I am a believer!"

"Oh Lord! You mean I have two to cope with? Are we going to sit around the fire at night and tell spook stories?"

"Now you just hush-up," Melba scolded, "I've just been trying to help her see her way through a few things. Go get cleaned up and I'll get dinner ready. This girl is ready for one of my home cooked meals. Just look how thin she is. We need to put some meat on her bones before she starts working herself to death."

He gave her a hug and winked at Carol, dashed off and returned quickly. "Come on we can sit on the porch while mom is cooking. We have some catching up to do."

As they sat together on the porch swing listening to the night sounds of crickets and tree frogs, Carol said, "Just listen to that, it has been years since I have heard that sound. It brings back many memories. I have grown accustomed to the city sounds of sirens, helicopters, traffic and horns blowing. This is nice. I'm glad you asked me to stay with you. Melba is right about that old house; it has its ghosts!"

Paul was silent for awhile, "You sound like mom and the folks in town talking about the Nelson's ghosts. Staying there will not be easy for you. Looking back is difficult and you'll have memories of your childhood and the days you spent there with your mother and father. And while you are remembering, don't forget about us, swimming, boating and fishing. How long has it been since you have seen a fish anyplace other than on a plate in front of you?"

"Oh Lord, I haven't had a fishing rod in my hands since I last fished with you. Those were wonderful days, the old swimming hole and the fishing. That's how long it's been."

"Before you start with that house and whatever else you have in mind, I hope you will take a little time to relax and allow us to have time together. I am in hopes you will decide to stay and take up where we left off. Miracles do happen! That you are here is proof of that! Don't break my heart and decide to sell and leave again."

She laid her head on his shoulder, "How does this feel to you? Does it feel like I am going to run away? To tell you the truth I wish I didn't have the house to contend with. Nevertheless, it is mine. My grandfather gave it to me and I must decide on what to do with it. If only he had written to me and told me what was on his mind. Perhaps something in the house will point the way for me. You are a lawyer and I may need your help. I am very surprised you were not expecting to see me! Were you not involved in the estate settlement? My grandfather knew you and liked you- and teased me every time he saw us together: 'Nice young man,' he would say and grin."

"That's funny! I never knew he even noticed me. Your grandfather and I were friends but he didn't do business with me. I doubt he had much faith in my ability. Your grandfather had a brilliant mind, built himself an empire and most all of his investments were done through out of town firms. I know nothing about his investments or business, none whatsoever. His estate was handled by a bigger firm than mine and I am not privy to the details. I could try to investigate but, until now, I haven't felt the need to do so. However, I am at your disposal and if there is anything I can do, I am here for you."

"The reason I asked is, I know he has a grandson and I am curious as to why he chose me as his heir. Without question, I feel sure that if there are any complaints I will hear about them."

"As a lawyer, I can tell you this; if your cousin's name was not in the trust left to you, he cannot contest it. The firm that notified you of your inheritance will give you any information you may need. If you are worried about his other heirs they can clear it up for you. Your grandfather bought and sold properties and no doubt invested highly in the market. I suspect he left much more to his grandson than he has to you. He was in business with his son, your cousin's father. I know about some of their housing projects in and around New York. He may have left a separate trust to him and any other heirs he may have had."

"You are right," Carol replied, "and if he has any complaints he will probably show up here. If so, it should be very interesting. I haven't seen him since we were kids, on holidays, when they visited grandma and grandpa. Like you, he will not know who I am. Time does change us! We age and our character also changes, yet, it does not seem to have changed you!"

"I thank you. My mirror does not agree. Still, I am the same person, older and hopefully wiser. You, my dear Carol, have improved with time. You were a freckle faced beauty and you are even more beautiful now."

"Paul, I could easily get caught up in our romance and forget about all else. Your nearness makes it difficult for me to keep my mind on my reason for being here. You must allow me to think. I need to talk about the house. It has such a quiet regal beauty. I had a feeling the walls were talking to me. The years have not changed it. Everything has remained the same. It is as if nothing has been touched or moved. I remember the pictures on the mantel and grandmother's clothing is in the upstairs closet. I did not open any drawers but I imagine they are full with everything folded neatly and in place. I have no idea where to begin. I will need help because there is much to be done. It's possible neither Gertie or her daughter will want to work after the sun goes down. Since Gertie says she has seen ghosts in the place, who knows? If the place is spooked I may have trouble getting anyone to work for me."

"Oh yes, I have heard about the ghosts! Some of the townspeople are saying the same thing." He chuckled, "People are funny! Ghosts or no ghosts, why don't you stay with us while getting everything worked out?"

She tucked her hand under his and placed her other hand on top, "I do appreciate this Paul! You have always been good to me, even when we were growing up. A little shy and always a gentleman. I remember the first prom you took me to, you walked me to the door and were too shy to kiss me goodnight."

"Oh yes, I remember! Since then, I have changed." An awkward moment followed and he continued. "I was heartbroken when you left and sure I would never see you again. I expected you to find someone else, get married and have children. Now you are here and to learn you are still single makes me happy."

"The bad penny always returns! I am also happy to find you are still single. It is as if we have never been apart. Call it fate; some unseen force has brought us together again. You have remained with me through the years, always in my thoughts and in my heart. I knew this day would come, even though I did not know where you were or if you were married. I never asked my grandfather. I should have asked him about you, but if I had learned you were married it would have made me unhappy." She blushed. "Forgive me for being so honest and forward."

He could feel her warmth against him and replied, "What is there to forgive? You have made it easy for me to say the things I should have said years ago. I turned you loose and tried to put you out of my mind but you were always there. Now fate has brought you back to me and I can say the things I was unable to say in my simple youth. When you left with your parents, I wanted to say don't go, stay with me. But I couldn't say it, the words wouldn't come. I was too young and had nothing to offer. I can still see you waving out the window with tears in your eyes. I felt it was the end and there would be no tomorrow for us. I determined the only way to get you back was to study, work hard and become a lawyer, then we could marry and be together forever. For a year or so you wrote to me often, yet our letters began to feel empty, not enough was said. We both talked about how life was treating us and what we were doing but we did not talk about our need for one another. Finally the time came when I thought you had moved on. We both still had growing to do. I dated, but no one meant anything to me. I tried to see in others what I saw in you but it never happened. I love you Carol, more than you can possibly understand. I am so thankful you have returned. However, I am sorry your grandfather had to die in order for me to see you again."

"It is hard for me to accept his death, yet I believe it was the unseen hand of God and my dear grandfather who planned and did this in order to bring me back to you. Tell me, do you believe his death was from natural causes? He wrote to me often and always sounded in high spirits. Not once did it occur to me that he might be ill because he never complained, except his letters grew sad when Grandma died."

"He was an old man, Carol. He did not have a heart attack as some choose to believe. He just went to bed one night and went to sleep. There were no substances in his blood to show he had taken an overdose or that he had been given anything to bring about his death. He once said he had a few drinks before retiring in order to rest. Who knows? Perhaps it was his way of combating his loneliness. He did miss your grandmother and being alone for so many years must have been difficult."

"It makes my heart ache to think about it. Now here I am the heir to his estate and heaven only knows what I will find in that old house."

Melba called, "Are you two ready for a good old fashioned dinner? If you are, it's on the table so come on in and get started. I bet you have forgotten how good old country style food taste. Help yourself to everything and eat all you want. I know you are both hungry."

"As happy as I am to be here, I should not be hungry but I am! We have so much to catch up on I would like to stay awake all night and talk. However, I am afraid after dinner I will head in for the night. It has been a very long day and I am tired. Tomorrow will be a decision making day with much work."

"Of course,"Paul agreed and held her hand while saying the blessing. "You are home, feel free to do things your way. We understand. And if there is anything we can do to help, you let us know."

"Yes, I am home. It is as if I have never been away."

After dinner she offered to help clear the table and clean the dishes but Melba would not allow it, "You take yourself to bed and rest."

"Okay, I'm gone, and I thank you." She gave Paul a long meaningful look, put her hand on his face and said goodnight. Completely fatigued, she crawled into bed, crossed herself, said her prayers and waited for sleep to come but it did not come easily. It had been an eventful day and evening, and Paul's nearness brought renewed hope. Nevertheless, with so much work ahead of her she could not allow herself to think of romance. Where should she begin and what would the future bring? She punched at her pillow and prayed for assistance, "God show me the way."

Morning found Melba in the kitchen and ready to stack Carol's plate with bacon and eggs, toast, fried grits and a cup of coffee. "Good morning honey, Paul has already left. He said I was to make sure you had a big breakfast to get you started."

"This is a really big breakfast! I can't do this everyday! I'll be as big as a barn. Tell me where Gertie lives and I'll eat and be out of here. I pray she will help me as she knows that old house better than anyone."

"When you leave here head out to the big house and keep going. She lives a mile on down the road in the black neighborhood. She doesn't have to live there because in today's world she could live anyplace, but some of the older blacks choose to remain in areas with their own. Gertie is part of the old world and that's where you will find her."

Carol finished her breakfast, gave Melba a hug and left. She found the little tumble down grocery store with sale signs in the window and parked, got out and went in, looked around and ask if someone could tell her where Gertie lived. A fat little lady stepped out from behind one of the shelves, "My Lord! Is that you Miss Carol? Jus look at you! All gowed up! You is found what you's lookin for, I'is your fat little ole Gertie!"

Carol threw her arms around her. "You haven't changed, not one little bit! Still a little butterball of joy. I am so happy to see you!"

"Tha's me! A little butterball. You looks jus like you mama! Now what can ole Gertie be doin fo you? What you doin here, no how?"

"Sit with me in the car and I'll tell you."

Gertie got into the car exclaiming about

how grand it was. "Look like you done got you a good man! This a mighty fine car!"

"No man Gertie. Hard work bought this car for me. What brings me here is the news of my grandfather's death! It makes me sad. I have missed him and my grandma ever since the day we moved away. It doesn't feel the same to be here without them. Grandpa left me his house and the land and I am here trying to decide what to do with it. It has been closed a very long time and I can't stay in it until it has been cleaned and everything has been gone through. And Gertie, that's why I have come looking for you. I need help. Will you help me?"

Gertie's eyes grew wide, "I don't know bout that Miss Carol! That old house scares me. It got ghosts! When the sun go down they starts movin round! I'is see'd em! I don't think I'is the right one for you. Git some white folk. They's plenty in town does that kind of work. Git one of them."

"I could Gertie, but I don't want them, I want you! No one knows that house better than you. You worked for my grandpa and grandma for as long as I can remember."

"I understands, but I'is scared of that old place. I don't think I can do it! I ain't been in it affa the day I found your granddaddy dead. I most died when I see'd him. I'is scared!"

"Well Gertie, I wouldn't expect you to be there without me. I would be in every room with you and you would not be there at night. Think about if Gertie! I would never leave you there by yourself. If I promise, will you consider working with me and for me? I will pay you as much as you want!"

Gertie sat mumbling and mulling it over in her mind. She needed money, jobs were hard for her to get; she was old and nobody wanted her. Carol could almost hear her thinking. "Hum-mm," She rolled her eyes, "I jus cain't say. Could you pays me ten dollars an hour? Tha's what white folks gits."

"Yes, Gertie, I will pay you ten dollars an hour. Some days will be shorter than others. It will depend on how much we can get done in a day. I really don't know where to begin. I will be depending very much on you. The part of the house you are most afraid of is the upstairs, am I right?"

"Yes, you right! Tha's where all them ghosts hang out. I'is shaking in my shoes jus thinkin bout it!"

Carol laughed, "Gertie, you are funny! I want to tell you something about ghosts. There are good ones and bad ones. Now you knew my grandpa and grandma and if their ghosts are in that house, they are good ones. So you are not to worry or be afraid. I'll handle that department. I have had allot of dealings with ghosts!"

"You ain't a'scared ov'em?"

"Of course not! If there are any bad ones there, what could they do to me? Nothing!"

"Oh, don't be too sure bout that Miss Carol. I'is heard stories!"

"Well don't you pay any attention to the

stories you have heard. If there are any bad ghosts in the house I will chase them out."

"I ain't never heard'a chasin no ghosts out of no place. Is you sure you can do that? Is you a witch?"

Laughing, Carol replied,"No Gertie, I am not a witch. You have known me since I was a little girl. Do I look like a witch? Was I a witch then? I may look different but I am not. I am just older and wiser."

"Well you done change since you is livin with them city folk!"

"Gertie, I am the same person. I have not changed. Anyone can chase out a ghost. All you have to do is say: I don't know you and I do not want you here, so go! Get out!"

"You means I can do that too?"

"Yes, you can! Now what do you say? Do you want to help me or not? I promise to stay in the same room with you full time."

"In that case, I can try. I'is an ole lady you know and gittin up them stairs ain't easy for me. If it be too much, would you let my grand-baby work for you?"

"Yes, of course, but I hope you can do it. Tomorrow I will pick you up and take you with me to the house. How about eight o'clock in the morning? How does that sound to you?"

"I won't be sleepin a wink tonight, but I be ready an shakin in my shoes!"

Carol laughed, gave her a hug and said, "You are not to worry! That old house and its ghosts will love you. Our lives make a circle and if we have lived a happy life a part of us is left behind. Now you know my grandparents were very much in love and lived a happy life. They left nothing in that house but happiness, so smile Gertie, this is going to be fun!" One more hug and she left Gertie shaking in her shoes.

"Melba was waiting and ready for all the news and had plenty of her own to tell."

"Well Melba, everything went fine. Gertie is going to work for me. However, if she finds it too difficult, her granddaughter will. Of course Gertie is a bit afraid of the house because she is sure it is full of ghosts. I assured her I would be in each room with her at all times and she had nothing to fear. Still, she says she may be too old for climbing stairs and if she can't make it would I consent to having her granddaughter work for me. I agreed, so it's settled! You should have seen how her eyes lit up when she saw my car. She said I must have me a fine man. Now, that's my news! What are you dying to tell me?"

"Come on in honey and sit while I figure out what to fix us for dinner. Have you had anything? If not I'll make you a sandwich and talk."

"I would love a sandwich! I completely forgot about lunch. I didn't even go to the old house today, thought tomorrow would be soon enough."

"I've got some nice ham here, how would that be, and maybe a glass of milk?"

"Wonderful, sounds great! If there is one thing I like to do, it's eat!"

Melba fixed the sandwich, added some chips, pickles and milk, placed it on the table in front of her, sat down and began to talk. "Well, let me tell you honey, this town is buzzing since learning you are here. I don't know how many phone calls I have had! And Lord, but I have been answering questions! Everyone wants to know how long you plan to be in town and if you are going to sell your grandfather's house. On top of that, invitations have flooded in wanting us to all to come to dinner. Kenneth Dobbs mother, Eunice, is anxious to have us. I think you must have dated him once in high school. He's unmarried and she has been trying to push him off on every other girl in town. Nice looking and no personality, remember him?"

"I surely do! He was very awkward and stepped all over my toes. I went with him once only because Paul didn't ask me. That was in our Freshmen year. Paul took me to all the others." She laughed, "Just picture her expression when she sees me now! I'm still the same person but I have changed the way I dress and may seem different to everyone."

"I didn't accept anything. I thought you and Paul should do the deciding. The main thing is, they are all curious about what you plan to do with your grandfather's old house. I could tell them nothing." She chuckled, "I'm sure they think I am holding out... I just love it!"

"You could not possibly know what my plans are as it is too soon for me to know! I hope to find a note or something from him in his desk, something that may give me a clue as to what he expects me to do with his house and property. There might be something in his safe deposit box at the bank. It must have been opened upon his death and as long as it did not contain money nothing could be removed. I should have done that today but I honestly did not give it a thought. I'm anxious to acquaint myself again with the house. I went there many times with my mom and dad, but I was young and did not give much thought to my surroundings. Daddy loved his father."

She sipped her coffee and thought for a moment. "Melba, what surprises me is, I have not heard from my uncle's son, Chad. Dad's brother died shortly after my father passed. One would think his son would question why the place was left to me. I'm expecting some fall out. I wonder if he knows I am here! If his lawyer is keeping track of things he probably does. My grandfather must have left something to him, but if he did it was not in my copy of the trust. I hate to think about it. He must hate me!"

"In time," Melba mused, "you will know! When it comes to death and money people are greedy."

"The truth is I feel guilty for owning it. Granddaddy had two sons and I find it odd he left it to me. Nonetheless, it is mine and I must decide what to do with it. Of course if there is anything in it that Chad would like to have, I will certainly see that he gets it. I hope he doesn't come here and try to take me to court."

"You need not worry about that," Melba replied. "If he does, Paul will take care of you. He won't let anyone take advantage of you."

"I doubt that will be necessary Melba. I don't think my cousin can do anything about my inheritance. If it had been left to me in a will he might be able to contest it, but it is not. I feel sure my grandfather left him plenty because his father and my grandfather were in business together. When Chad's father died he must have inherited plenty from his father's part of the business. I suspect he is the same kind of shrewd business man as his father, usually the apple doesn't fall far from the tree. I should not make assumptions as I don't know him. Did he come to the funeral?"

"Oh my yes! He came! I expected to see you, but you didn't come. He stayed at the hotel and may have spent a few days out at the house going through things, I don't know. He was a bit uppity and we did not get well acquainted. Of course none of us knew the house had been left to you and it seemed only natural that he would be looking through things at your grandfather's home. We thought he might have a memorial for him out there but he didn't. He came, stayed at the hotel long enough for the funeral and left a couple of days later. Most everyone your grandfather knew was graveside when he was buried and all expressed their condolences, but he did not extend himself and everyone thought he was strange. Paul can tell you more about it than I. Your grandfather had prearranged his burial with the funeral home, so there was nothing for Chad to do. Since the house was left to you, I question why he even went near it? Should it not have had a lock on it?"

"Yes it should, but I suppose since he was the only blood relative who showed up at his funeral the authorities did not question him. It really doesn't matter to me. I inherited the house and land which is more than I ever expected. I don't care about anything else. I am still in shock over inheriting. I would have come to the funeral, had I known he died. I knew nothing until informed of my inheritance."

"You are like your mother. There was not a greedy bone in her. I will never understand why you all left here."

"It wasn't something my mother wanted. Daddy was not like his father or his brother Tim. He was not a business man. Daddy was happy working for the other fellow. He didn't have a head for business. He was a tailor and should have been in business for himself but he didn't want that. Instead, we went to California and he found work in a Hollywood department store altering and making suits for prominent people. His work was so good it afforded him a lifetime job without worry, no bookkeeping, no hiring or firing, no goods to order and no inventory for him to keep. It was the perfect job for him, a job without headaches and time to live.

My grandfather offered to set him up with a business here in town but it was not the kind of life dad wanted, and I am not sorry! We had a beautiful life and home. Mom and dad adored each other and we were a very happy family until mother's death. After that the joy left my father. He continued to work but his life really ended when he lost her. One day while at work he had a heart attack and died. My life has not been the same without them!" Tears fell from her eyes. "Oh I am sorry, I didn't mean to do that! I don't want to depress you."

"Oh honey, I'm glad you told me all this. If you hadn't, in time I would have dragged it out of you. Paul warned me to not ask too many questions. He said if you wanted me to know about your life you would tell me. He was right. Now then, let's decide what to have for dinner."

"Melba! I've just finished this sandwich! How can I think of dinner?"

"You will be hungry by tonight! I think I will make an old fashioned meat loaf, some lyonnaised potatoes, creamed green peas and caramelized carrots and a green salad. For dessert I have a pineapple upside down cake."

"Oh Lord! By the time I've finished with grandpa's house I'm going to be as big as the house! It's been a very long time since I've had so much good food."

"Why don't you go take a little nap while I do my cooking. It will be awhile before Paul gets home. I know your head must be spinning. You have been at it all day long. A nice warm bath and a little rest will do you good."

"Okay Melba, you've talked me into it!" She went to her room, ran a bath and soaked in the nice warm water. How could she rest with so much to think about? Tomorrow would be the real beginning. After her bath she fell across the bed and slept and dreamed. In her dreams she saw herself searching, going from room to room in her grandfather's house. Around three she awoke with a start, pulled on a velvet jump suit and headed for the kitchen. Melba had said she would be hungry by dinner and she was. The aroma of food spices awakened her appetite.

Melba greeted her excitedly, "Oh boy, guess who's coming to dinner?"

"I would not dare to venture a guess. Tell me quickly because I can see you can hardly wait."

"You are not going to believe! Paul called from the office and told me! It's your cousin! He has checked into our fabulous hotel. Somehow, he must have learned that you were here."

"His lawyers probably told him. Wonder what he is after? Surely didn't waste any time getting here, did he? This should be interesting! Of course if his father was alive that old house may have gone to him and I suppose Chad is as anxious as everyone else to know what I plan to do with it and the land. Isn't this interesting? Who would have thought so much intrigue would surround that house?"

"Well, I was not expecting an extra guest. Thank heavens I always cook too much. Could you set the dining room table for me. You will fine my best dinnerware in the china closet and in one of the drawers the silverware. We don't want your cousin to think we are peasants!"

"Now Melba, let us not prejudge."

They both laughed and got busy. "I suppose I should change into something less casual but I'm not going to do it. He is a surprise guest and I will stay just as I am."

"And you well should. You look beautiful in that rose colored outfit and we are not going to put on airs for him! Except in the dining room," she giggled. "I knew him when he was a little boy. He is not one bit better than us, even if his father and grandfather were filthy rich."

Carol gave Melba a hug. "I love you. The years have not changed you."

The door opened and Paul walked in. "I see you two are at it. Has mom filled you in on the news of our surprise guest? Guess your cousin is anxious to see you."

"Hello yourself Paul! That's some kind of a greeting! You are supposed to give us a hug or kiss before you start asking questions. But to answer your question, I just got the latest with 'guess who's coming to dinner!'I took a nap and meanwhile she has been in this kitchen working.

Paul laughed, "You two are just alike!" He gave Melba a kiss, "I would kiss you, too, but I don't want the neighbors to talk!"

Carol leaned forward, "Go ahead, give me one right here on my lips and let them talk."

He did, and paused to look into her eyes. She smiled, blushed and pulled away as the old fire kindled up. "Did my cousin say what time he would be arriving?"

"Yes. I told him to come early. He will be here at six. I'll take him into the living room and we can all have a cocktail before dinner. A drink will loosen him enough for comfort."

"Is he that stuffy? My uncle must have been a stuffed-shirt! If so, he was nothing like my dad. No wonder they didn't get along! Born of the same parents and completely different. My dad was down to earth and a joy to be with, as was my grandfather."She stopped and watched Paul's eyes surveying her."What? You don't like what I'm wearing?"

"On the contrary, you look beautiful and comfortable. That color is perfect for you, makes your cheeks look all rosy and your eyes bluer than blue. I wouldn't change a thing."

Melba was listening but said nothing. It was plain to see they were renewing their long denied feelings for one another. She wondered why they had never corresponded. No matter, because it looked as if the flame was still there and she liked it.

"Why don't you two go into the living room and get the bar set up. Everything is under control in here. He may turn up his nose at my meatloaf. It may be a little country for him but that's what happens when one arrives unexpectedly. He probably dines out in all those highfalutin restaurants in New York."

"If he doesn't like your meatloaf," Paul replied, "there is something very wrong with him. We do not have to cater to his taste or his way of living. This is our home and he is lucky to be invited." He pinched her cheek, "So don't you worry old dear. If he wants to return the favor we will be happy to accept. I am sure as soon as the news of his arrival travels around town all kinds of invitations will come rushing in. Come on Carol let's get a little libation before the fun begins."

Melba sent a knowing look to Carol and laughed: "The news is already out. Our phone has been ringing all day! Everyone in town has invited us to dinner. I thought it was because of Carol, now I see it is because of both. Guess the town thinks they are in cahoots and they want to know what is going on! This should be fun!"

"If you say so mom!" He put his arm around Carol and they walked together into the living room. "We need to get a head start before company arrives," he said, and pulling her to him he kissed her, passionately, "and that's for starters."

Carol caught her breath, and said, "Nice start."

"Do you want us to bring you one mom?"

"Please do! I need a booster!"

"That's my mom! She is always ready for anything."

"Me too! Make me a Vodka Tonic, I can see I will need a couple of drinks to get me through this evening of meeting up with my cousin." He pulled her close and kissed her again. "Better turn me loose," she whispered, cleared her throat and in a louder voice, exclaimed, "my curiosity is killing me!   Melba told me he was here for the funeral and spent time at the house. How did he managed that? What is he after?"

Melba called, "Companies here!"

"Great timing," Paul grumbled, released her and went to welcome her cousin.

Chad, was tall, handsome and dressed expensively casual, wearing a cashmere sweater, cropped trousers and soft shoes. For a moment Carol was taken aback by his resemblance to her father. His hair, obviously styled, made him look as if he had stepped out of a page of Esquire. One could tell at a glance he thought himself to be quite dashing and a cut above the average man. Carol held out her hand when introduced and he held it for a moment saying, "At last we meet, I have heard much about you dear cousin but I did not expect to find such a beauty."

She pulled her hand away, sipped at her drink and searchingly eyed him. "I am equally surprised! The resemblance between you and my father in his earlier years is remarkable. I don't remember your father very well as I seldom saw him. Did he and my father look alike?"

"Please make yourself comfortable,"Paul suggested, "and while you two get acquainted I'll mix you a cocktail. We have a little of everything. What would you like?"

"I would love a glass of wine, if you have it."

"We do. What is your preference? We are

having meat for dinner. Mom has made one of her fantastic meatloaf specialties and I suggest you try a glass of Montoya Reserve Cabernet; it will enhance the flavor."

"Yes, it sounds wonderful. Meatloaf! I can't remember when I last dined on meatloaf! My dining habits have changed greatly since my childhood. I suppose I am a city person. As you know my father left here when he was young, met my mother and married in the city. My mother was not an around the home kind of housewife and we seldom had family style dinners. Of course when we entertained clients it was necessary. Your invitation surprised and pleased me because it also included a chance to acquaint me with my cousin, the heir to my grandfather's large and beautiful estate."

Carol found her voice, "He was also my grandfather! As for the size of the estate, at this point I have no idea how large it is. I have only been here a few short days. Your arrival is quite a surprise. What brings you here? I heard you attended our grandfather's funeral. How well did you know him? Did you and your father often visit him?"

"Not often. I knew him but we were not close. However, my father filled me in on all his eccentricities."

Carol's hair bristled, "I beg your pardon! Our grandfather was not an eccentric! He was a gloriously down to earth intelligent loving man who amassed himself a fortune. He bought and sold property because he loved the earth and he loved this town. Most of all, he loved his wife and children. He also did well for your father as they were in business together. It is my understanding, he taught your father everything about real-estate buying and selling and they joined forces. Do not make disparaging remarks about him! If you do, you and I will not get along!"

Both Paul and Chad were surprised at her sudden outburst. Not one to mince words, she also let it be known she did not need the estate left to her by her grandfather or his money. She was quite happy in her little pond. His words had struck a nerve and in an instant she knew his visit was not by chance. He had come with an ulterior motive.

She continued, "To know our grandfather and our grandmother was to love them. They shared a very deep love, like that of my mother and father. Our grandfather was not greedy! He started with nothing, worked hard and proudly built himself an empire. He cared about his fellow man and was there for those who were less fortunate. He had two sons and they were not alike, your father and mine. My father was not money conscious or greedy. He preferred his freedom to live and love without the worry that comes with money. He had peace of mind, love and a comfortable living."

Chad downed his glass of wine and asked for another. "I'm sorry my dear, I certainly did not mean to sound disrespectful. I can only go by the things my father has said about his father, our grandfather."

"Well your father should have never said our grandfather was an eccentric! Was it not he who reared and educated your father? Was it not he who gave him the opportunities to advance in the business world? Without his father, what would he have been? You need to ask yourself these questions! Never look down you nose at our grandfather! Do not disrespect the man who has moved mountains to make it possible for you to be a rich man today! Perhaps a little trip around the estate with me will give you insight into a beautiful past. But be aware of the unseen forces that haunt his mansion! You may not be welcomed!"

"Oh my! Are you trying to tell me the place is haunted! Surely you do not believe in all that voodoo haunting fantasizing?"

She laughed and asked for another drink. "Who knows? You may become a believer! It is written: 'Believe in the seen and unseen.' Or do you not believe in the omnipotent? Tell me, what do you believe in?"

"Well, I can see this trip is going to be much more interesting than expected! To answer your question, I am an agnostic. To me, seeing is believing!"

"And what do you think of the universe?" she asked, "Did man create it? What do you see out there that you believe exist? From whence did we come? Have you an answer? If so, I am sure the world would love to know about it!"

Melba entered, glass in her hand and looking for a refill. "You all are in here enjoying drinks while I am slaving in the kitchen. Fill my glass and I will fill your stomachs!"

Carol got up, put her arms around Melba, and said, "Perfect timing, I am starving and can hardly wait for some of your wonderful down home cooking." She sent a meaningful glance at Chad. "I think our guest is in for a surprise! He is out of touch with country pleasures."

Melba looked from one to the other, "I think I must have missed something. Well let us not dilly-dally, let us eat while it is hot."

Paul put his arm around Carol's waist and gave her a squeeze. He could feel her anger. "May I escort you to the dining room my dear?" And turning to Chad, "Would you escort mom, she will tell you which place is yours. You are in for a treat," he said, grinning devilishly, "with mom's gourmet meatloaf!"

The table was set with Melba's best china and silverware, bread plates and cut-glass water and wine glasses. In the center of the table was a platter of sliced, ready to serve meatloaf, a bread warmer filled with hot-cross buns and serving dishes filled with lyonnaised potatoes, creamed green beans, caramelized carrots and a fresh green salad. All were passed around the table, family style from one to the other. Paul poured the wine and made a toast, after which Carol reached for the hands of those on either side of her and said the blessing.

Unaccustomed to such simple pleasures, Chad was at a total loss. He blushed, "I have never sat at a table with people like you and I have never heard a blessing. This is all very new to me and wonderful! I thank you so much for inviting me."

Carol's opinion of him softened. It was odd to see someone so out of touch with the real world. He had missed the simple pleasures in life. Happily filling his plate with everything, he ate and went back for seconds.

"Melba," he exclaimed, "you have won me over! I have never had anything as good as your meatloaf! And Paul, the wine is excellent. I have been here in the past but it was not the same. Mother was with us and we stayed stayed at the mansion with grandma and grandpa. Grandfather, as I recall, had many servants and dining was quite formal. Our grandmother was a beautiful lady who did seem to enjoy elegant entertaining. However, our visits were few and far between so I never got to know them well."

Melba smiled, "Your grandmother was dignified and elegant but she was also the salt of the earth. She was not at all highbrowed. She enjoyed entertaining and the finer things in life and she also enjoyed tilting a little glass of spirits." She laughed and tossed him a defiant look, "Now we have a real treat for dessert. "I made a pineapple upside down cake and I hope you like pineapple!"

Ignoring the threat in her eyes, Chad smiled, "I think I will enjoy anything you have to offer. And if you have coffee, I would love a cup of coffee with the cake."

"Would I serve cake without it?"

While having their dessert and coffee, Carol asked, "Tell me, exactly why are you here in our fair city? You surely did not come for the soul purpose of meeting me. I feel sure that you have also inherited a great deal from our grandfather and now have something in mind concerning my inheritance."

He smiled, "You are quick to the point. I thought you would get around to asking, but let us not spoil a beautiful evening with shop talk. I am not going to leave town right away. I was in hopes of spending a few nights in the old mansion. My memory of it is vague. I thought we might sit by the fireplace and get to know each other."

Carol laughed, "Well then, I think you are going to be here for quite some time. The house has been closed and is in need of repair and cleaning. I have not had a chance to explore it in its entirety. I am in hopes of going through it tomorrow with Gertie. She is the lady who took care of the house and our grandfather before he died. She is not young and I do not expect things to move quickly. If you are living at the hotel, I suggest you make yourself comfortable and be ready for a long wait."

Paul gave thought to inviting him to stay with them but one glance in Melba's direction quickly changed his mind. Attempting to change the subject, he said, "Our phone has been ringing off the hook and, sufficed to say, while here you will not starve. It seems that everyone in town is anxious to have all of us to dinner. It looks as if mom will not be spending much of her time in the kitchen. Pity, because I doubt you will find the dining as pleasurable as you have found it here. We do not stand on the kind of decorum others find so necessary. Some will be quite formal and boring."

Chad looked at everyone, "It looks as if this is going to be a very eventful trip. I surely did not expect anything like this. It has been a long evening and you must be tired. Paul, I will call on the morrow at your office and we can chat. I will then fill my days with some rides around Grandfather's properties. I am told there is much to be seen."

Carol grasped the hidden meaning in his words and pretended not to notice. "Should you be inclined," she offered, "come by the house and I can show you through the rooms. It is a beautiful historical mansion! There are few like it still standing. It echos the genteel refinement of the past and it should never be destroyed. But do not forget my warning; you may hear voices or be touched by the unseen!"

He laughed, "I do not believe in ghosts. If possible, I am sure you would conjure up a few and call them in to frighten me away."

"Just wait and see! As you have said, if you cannot see something, you do not believe it is there. You laugh now because you believe in nothing! If you had any kind of faith you would believe in the unseen. But you are a doubting Thomas. You can stand on the shore and cannot see the fish beneath the surface, yet you know they are there! I doubt you believe in miracles, yet you are here through the miracle of birth. Your reaction to the unseen, will greatly please me."

"You will not have that pleasure, as I repeat, I am an agnostic. I must see to believe! Take a picture of your ghosts and I might agree with you!"

"Until now you had not heard a blessing, but since you have, do you not think it is right for us to give thanks for all we have?"

"Well Carol, I am thankful for everything I have. And I am thankful for this lovely dinner I have enjoyed with you all. It is late and I must part. You have given me much to think about."

Paul walked him to his car and said, "I believe you have met your match. Carol is not to be trifled with. I have known her all my life. We went together in high school and when your uncle moved them to the coast it broke my heart. She was different then, freckle faced and shy. She no longer has freckles and she is not shy. She grew strong and determined. You have just learned she is honest, forthright and does not hide her feelings or pull her punches. She will get right to the point with you and will expect the same from you and others, so be prepared. Like her mother, she is clairvoyant. You may not believe in clairvoyance, but I do."

"A strange thing for a lawyer to say and I will not argue the point with you. I will see you tomorrow."

As Paul entered the house he caught the

expression on both lady's faces.

"He is here for a reason," Carol said. "He is after something and I am going to stay on my toes. He is deceptively nice. Something is going on behind those blue eyes. He has dollar signs in place of pupils in his eyes. He inherited, but it is not enough. He wants everything! Wait here for a minute."

She went to her room and returned. "Look this over tonight. It is my grandfather's trust and how he left things to me. Please look it over very carefully and see if there are any loopholes in it. Chad inherited from his father, and our grandfather would not have overlooked him. Perhaps he made a separate trust for Chad. If so, he didn't get all that he wanted! I believe you know me well enough to know I am not greedy. Nonetheless, I do not like the feeling I am getting from my dear cousin. Not in my wildest dreams did I ever expect to inherit anything! When my father died there was not much to inherit except the little house we had and I still have it! It is filled with memories of love and happiness. I can take care of myself, I have all a person could want or need in life. My grandfather left me this place and property for a reason and I intend to find out what that reason is! If he had wanted Chad to have it, he would have left it to him! If he had wanted his son to have it, he would have left it to him years ago. My dear old grandfather was a thinking man and for some reason he did no want it left to that side of his family."

"Carol honey, you said you have all you need, does that include me?"

"Yes, I need you more than anything else," she answered and gave him a kiss.

"I will give all this a very close look, but I cannot for the life of me see where there is anything Chad could do to take it away from you. I think you need sleep because you will be up with the dawn and out working your little tush off tomorrow. So give me another kiss and go to bed and get some rest."

"No, I think I should help Melba in the kitchen. She worked very hard making that wonderful dinner and she might like to talk with me for awhile and share a few of her cherished opinions. I'm sure she has a few."

A voice came from the other room, "Oh yes, I have a few but they can wait! I need to mull them around for awhile. We can talk in the morning. As for this kitchen, I would rather do all this by myself, it's easier that way. I can take my time and put things away. I know where everything goes and you don't. You do as Paul said and take yourself to bed."

Paul walked her to her door, held her close and kissed her goodnight. "Chad is very good looking, I'm glad he's not a kissing cousin! I'll see you in the morning."

Carol laughed out loud. "That is funny, Paul! Even if he was, he is too prissy for me! That man will find himself a well healed society lady. He may have a few lined up in New York. He is so into himself! Or did you notice?"

A voice from the kitchen, "I noticed!"

Paul answered, "Lord mother, how did you manage to hear that? Are you working or are you listening? Maybe we all need a night cap to aid us in raking cousin Chad over the coals."

"These hallways are short and although I am not young I am still not deaf my boy! Want me to stick some cotton in my ears?"

Carol laughed again, "Goodnight you two. As Chad said: I'll see you in the morrow!"

Morning found Melba in the kitchen, humming and cooking. She looked up as Carol entered. "There you are young lady. Paul had hoped to see you before he left for the office but in case your fancy cousin decided to make an early visit, he decided he should be there to meet him."

"I'm sorry I missed him. Just look at the time! I really over slept. Gertie will be anxiously waiting."

"Now don't you worry about Gertie, she won't mind if you are late. I have never seen Gertie in a hurry! Are you meeting her in the grocery store? If you are, you will find her talking and having a good time with all her friends. That grocery store is just like the barber shop. It's a hang out for all to catch up on the local gossip. You just sit yourself down while I fix you some bacon, eggs and fried grits. Once you start working you will probably forget to eat. I have made a lunch for you and Gertie to have while chasing ghosts. It's in this basket so don't forget to take it with you."

"You are a sweetheart Melba, and you are right. I would probably forget to eat. If Gertie is convinced she has seen ghosts in the house at night, she is going to be some kind of funny! I say, if she has seen lights in the place a curious someone has been sneaking in searching for something. The lights she saw might have been when Chad was here for the funeral. That sounds possible. He might have been there looking for deeds and things. Time will tell!"

Melba sat a plate of food and a cup of coffee on the table in front of Carol. "Now you eat every bite of that!"

"I will! It looks delicious. I'll make short work of it and be on my way. You really have me spoiled. I will never cook for myself again!"

A half hour later she was on her way, and Gertie was there waiting and not the least upset because she was late. "If we starts late it give my ole bones time! Ten is better to gits me ready for them ghosts!"

"Good idea Gertie, this country air made me sleep late. Staying with Paul and Melba makes me feel safe and happy. Now let's go!"

Gertie got out of the car and opened the gate, got back in and shivered. "I'is feelin them ghosts already!"

"You are not to worry Gertie, the ghosts love me because my granddaddy gave me this place. I think we are going to have fun! Melba made us a big lunch to have after we are through chasing ghosts."

She parked, they got out and Gertie hung close to her side. One foot on the first step and it creaked. Gertie stopped, "What was that?"

"Your foot on the step! For goodness sake Gertie, are you going to jump at every little noise you hear? These old houses are full of noises and around noon it will start to make other sounds. It is not unusual for the change of temperature to make these old places moan and groan. After awhile you will get used to it. Throughout the years while working for my grandpa and grandma you must have heard these sounds."

"No I ain't heard nothin like that! Guess I be too busy! But if I hears a moan, you gonna see my feet move cause I be gone!"

"We are going to be too busy for you to worry. Now put that lunch on the table and we will begin with the attic. We will start at the top and work our way down. How's that?"

"If you says so Miss Carol, but ain't much up there for you to find. Your grandma done went through the attic. Said she was too ole to worry bout all the junk up there. One day some mens git most everthin down and she had herself a yard sale. The whole neighborhood come scroungin. Oh but she love it! She gits a rockin chair and sits right out in the middle of the whole thing, jus laughin and visitin with all them folks!"Gertie bent over laughing, "Wish you coulda see'd her Miss Carol! She was in heaven. Your grandma was somethin else! I loved her to pieces!"

"Well Gertie, we are going up those stairs, anyway, something important might have been left up there. Now come on, don't be afraid, I am with you." She took Gertie's hand, held it and dragged her up the stairs. When they reached the top, Carol opened the door and stepped in and Gertie cautiously followed. One foot inside, Gertie froze and let out a wail that shook the rafters and turned and ran for the stairs.

"I tole you they's ghosts in this house!"

Unable to contain herself, Carol began to laugh.

"Ain't funny Miss Carol, I'is gone!"

Carol grabbed her shirt tail and stopped her. "Gertie, you get right back here and I will show you your ghost! Come on! I know you are going to love this one because you have seen it before."

Gertie shook her head and pulled in the other direction. "No mam! I see'd plenty!" Carol kept pulling and finally Gertie unwillingly returned and eased one foot into the room.

"Now," Carol said, "look at your ghost."

Gertie looked straight ahead, screamed again and began to laugh. Tears ran down her face and she bent over laughing, sat down on the steps, pointed at the ghost behind her, and said, "Miss Carol, it look like me!"

"That's because it is you! You are looking in a mirror!"

Gertie, again, looked over her shoulder and the ghost was sitting on the steps laughing. Screaming with laughter, she got up and neared the mirror. "I swear Miss Carol, I scared myself so bad I done wet my pants."

"If you see a ghost in every room we will never get this done! My grandma did a good job of emptying this attic. It is as bare as a dance hall. Wonder why she left this mirror? It is a very nice piece of furniture and could have been used in one of the rooms. The frame around it looks like rosewood." She put her hands on it and walked around it. "It is in perfect condition Gertie, even the mirror!" The back was neatly covered with material. "This is a beautiful relic." She ran her hand over the covering on the back and dust flew. "Come here Gertie. See if you can feel something under this."

Gertie reached out and put the palms of her hands on it and slowly felt along. "Yes'm, they is somethin."

"Let's get it out of there." Carol gave the material a tug and it ripped away revealing an envelope stuck to the back of the mirror. On it was written: For Carol, read this carefully while in the presence of no one. It concerns you and no one else.

"Can you beat that?" Gertie said. "Who you think done that? What do it say?"

"It says it is for me and I am to read it when I am alone. That means, after we have done a little cleaning I will take you home and return here to read it. I think I should be in granddaddy's study when I look it over."

"What? Why you gonna wait? Was me, I be lookin right now! Maybe you needs to look!"

"Gertie, it has been here for God only knows how long, so it can wait a little longer. I am as curious as you, but it will wait! Now let us get busy. How many rooms are on this floor?"

Gertie watched her tuck the envelope into her pocket."Um-um, you gonna wait. Um-um." She shook her head. "They's eight. Four on each side the hall and all got a bathroom. When they's young, they's used lots. Your grandma love parties. But she gits ole and they's no more parties, so she done close ever room. She did love dressin up an wearin all her fine jewelry an lacy stuff. She look like a flower, an she love lavender an smelt like it. No other lady hold no candle to her. Nice days Miss Carol. I wishes they's still here."

"Oh I can remember some of those parties because my mother and father insisted we join them. I was in high school when we moved and she had a big going away party for us. Mother loved her parties! My daddy was different and was not thrilled with them. He was a quiet man, and did not like their pompous ceremonial gatherings."

"Why you all move Miss Carol?"

"My grandfather tried to talk daddy into staying and offered to set him up in business, but daddy was determined to move. He did not want to be under the thumb of his father, even though he loved him very much. Daddy wanted a life of his own."

"Oh I members him, a fine lookin man! An you mama was pretty, jus like you!"

"Thank you Gertie. Now let's have a look in here." She opened a door into one of the bedrooms. "Just look at this! Did you do all this?" Everything was covered with sheets.

"Some!"

They began to remove the sheets in each bedroom. All the rooms had small sitting rooms, sliding doors and joining bathrooms. Four poster beds and rosewood dressers with large round mirrors. Centered in front of them were small dressing table chairs covered with needle point designs. Reflecting the splendor of the past, were tall rosewood chest of drawers and men's suit valets. The closets held extra linens, with tatting on the edges. All had to be removed and cleaned. The elaborate drapes and bedspreads of Toile, printed linen, indigo blue spoon-flower design must be cleaned and the windows washed.

Carol looked around and sighed, "Oh Gertie, we have a giant job ahead of us and we cannot do all this by ourselves. We will need added help, men with muscle for the heavy work. Do you know of others who will be willing to work for me? I do not want any shiftless lazy ones. I want men who will hop to when I say I want something done."

"Yes Mam! I does! How many does you wants?"

"Two strong men and two other ladies. Can your granddaughters help?"

"Yes, mam!"

"We cannot do all this at one time. We

will do one floor at a time. With luck we may be able to get the entire house done within six months. By then my pocket book will be empty and my savings will be gone."

"Sound like you's plannin on keepin this place! Everone been askin! Even the black folk."

"I am completely undecided. I can't think about it now. I want you to find me some honest workers, not thieves! If anyone is found stealing they will be fired. I will make a list of everything in the rooms and that includes any jewelry we may find."

"I understands. My boy and his'un need work an they's honest. They's got chillun to feed."

"Okay! We are off to a good start. Let's eat. Look in that basket and see what we have for lunch?"

"Yes, mam! I'is ready! I feels like I ain't done nothin!"

"Have you seen anymore ghosts Gertie?"

She laughed, "No I ain't! But I feels like somebody be watchin!"

"You are right! We are not alone! I told you these walls hold memories of many happy years, much love and glorious parties, so Gertie, you will continue to feel it. You are safe, nothing will bother you. This may be your shortest day of work. I must get myself a ledger in order to get the names of the people who are going to work for me. In it, I will write down the amount of hours worked each day. We have only been here for about five hours, today. Do you want me to pay you now or do you want to wait until the end of a week's work? You will be working broken hours for awhile because we are just starting."

"Yes mam, today. I needs the money."

"When I get the others working and know exactly what it is they will be doing, I will figure out their hours. We will not work tomorrow because I have things I must do in town. Tomorrow afternoon, around two, I will meet you at the grocery store and you can have the men there for me to hire. I will get their names and next day we will start. We won't work on Sundays because we all need to go to church and thank God for all our blessings. That will give us two days, Friday and maybe Saturday, and Sunday off. Then back to work Monday. Now, let's eat and I'll drive you home, okay?"

"It ain't far an I done walk to an from this old house more times I can count, so I'is gonna walk. It be like old times."

They dusted off the table in the kitchen and dug into the basket of food, sandwiches, potato salad, chips, soft drinks and pie."

Gertie smacked her lips, "Miss Carol, this a picnic! That Miss Melba know how to make a body happy! I ain't done a lick of work an it shame me to take you money but I needs it. White folk is takin our jobs. An they ain't no use for ole Gertie no more."

"Gertie, you are very needed not just for the work but for the memories of all the years I have missed by not living here. I look forward to my days with you. There may be some days when we won't work. I need the men to climb ladders, wash windows, and repair things that are broken. The chandeliers must be brought down and washed. That alone is a big job. Crystal, does not want to see soap, it takes away the luster. We have a big job ahead of us. The men will also do the lawns and the shrubbery. The garden needs care and plant food. The house must be painted and the walls repaired. I don't know where to begin. Today we have made a start and once we get going you can keep the girls working. You will be their boss."

Gertie smiled, "I'is that!" She had her lunch and Carol gave her fifty dollars. Her hands shook as she held the money, "Bless you Miss Carol. I knows God has sent you," she said, and went happily on her way.

Carol waited until she was out of sight then put her lunch aside, went into her grand-father's study, sat in his chair, leaned back and opened the envelope and began to read the words that were written with a shaky hand:

My very dear loving granddaughter, how I wish your father had not taken you and your dear mother away. James was so talented, such a fine tailor. He and his brother did not get along, did not see eye to eye and as long as his brother was here your father could not be. There was bad blood between them. It might have been because his brother had hoped to win your mother's heart. He tried to court her but she could see no one but James. She very kindly and politely let Timothy know he could never win her heart as she was in love his brother.

It had been my wish to one day leave this house and property to your father but God had other plans. Your father and your dear beautiful mother passed before I. I have lost too many of my loved ones and my heart is heavy. Therefore, because I could not bequeath it to them, I have left it to you.

My sight is failing and writing is difficult. Your grandmother must have had a premonition because when I asked her why she kept the old mirror, she said it would come in handy. I didn't know what she meant but the time came when I understood. There had to be a place in this house to hide my message and I remembered her words. I very carefully stuck it to the backside of the mirror and prayed you would be the one to find it. I feared you would not, but God has directed you to it. I dared not leave it in the safe deposit box for someone else to find.

I do not want this house destroyed. It is filled with love and joy. If you sit quietly and listen you will hear the voices of the past. When your dear grandmother died I promised her I would remain here and would not sell. The year that followed her death was difficult; I was depressed and grieving. I could not understand why God did not take me with her. Without her there was no life.

One evening while sitting in front of the fireplace watching the flames, reminiscing and feeling sorry for myself, I looked up and I saw lingering overhead, three tiny little diamonds. They compelled me to watch and pay attention.

When I finally found my voice, I asked, 'is that you love?' The little diamonds zoomed down close to me, hovered over me as if they were looking into my soul and I knew it was her. She was trying to make me happy. I held my hand up to her and said: 'if this is you, touch my hand.' The little diamonds, like eyes, came down and touched my hand. I very gently cupped my hand around them. A glow, like a small white cloud hovered there within my palm and I talked to her. From that moment on I was not alone. Every night I would look for her and she would come and comfort me. No words were spoken by her. I asked questions and tried to explain my plans. If they pleased her she would move around and come close in a kind of light. If I said something that displeased her, the eyes would appear amidst a dark cloud and I knew to drop that idea and find another.

And so it happened, when I was making out my trust she lingered and watched over me. Your father's brother, Timothy, died shortly after your father passed. Tim had a son, Chad, and I knew Tim had left his share of our joint business to him. My dear wife was not fond of Chad and since I could not leave my shares of the business to either of my sons, I asked if I should leave it to Chad as he was like his father and enjoyed the business world. She agreed. That left me with this house and property and I made my decision to bequeath it to you. When I told your grandmother I thought you should have it, bright streaks of light flashed around the room and danced around excitedly. I had made the right decision. It was after that I wrote this note and took it to the attic.

Your cousin Chad is wealthy. I and his father built an empire for him to inherit. I made a separate trust in order to leave him my shares of the business. I don't know much about him, except that his father spoiled him and gave him everything he wanted. He is good looking, well educated and well mannered; however, I would not trust him with this house. I trust you because you are your father's child.

It is a big house that has given us much happiness and I feel sure you will find a way to give some of the happiness we shared to others.

Before you make any decisions, I want you to sit by the fire and wait for us. We will tell you what to do. Do not get impatient while waiting because we will come. We will give you time to make up your mind and we will watch you begin. Then, one day when you think you have lost us and you don't know how to make up your mind, we will come.

This is a large estate with ten thousand acres of land, that's about sixteen square miles. You may not have the resources to take care of it. Between this estate and another there lives a very wealthy man by the name of Roy McFarland. Separating us is approximately six hundred acres of land that belongs to you. He has tried many times to buy it from me. He is a Scotsman with a very tight fist. He will come to you and make an offer. Make him wait, no matter how badly you need money, do not accept his first offer. He has ways of finding out when one is in a tight spot. Hold off, he will come to you with three offers. The last one will will make you rich. The land is very valuable but he will try to buy it for as little as possible. He can afford any price. Do not sell it for less than one million five hundred thousand dollars. The remaining property you will keep. There is where you will need our help deciding what is best for you and for others. By that time you may have someone in your life to help guide you.

Do not, under any circumstance, sell any property to Chad. I feel sure he will try to buy it. But do not sell to him! He has more money than he needs. This estate will bring you happiness, more than he will ever find with his wealth.

James, your father and mother, Edna Jane, found happiness without my help. And you will also find your happiness here, with just a little nudge from your old grandpa and grandma.

Take care my dear. We will come to you. Never tell anyone about us or this letter. If anyone heard of it they would say the old man was suffering from dementia and didn't know what he was doing. It would be used against you.

We love you. We are in the company of your mother and father and we are all looking down at you and watching over you. When you sit by the fire and look up you will see more than three little diamonds, you will see twelve and you will feel happy and secure. No one else will ever see us, unless it is someone who loves you as deeply as we all have loved. If the one who says he loves you, does not see us, beware."

Carol read and reread the letter. It gave her strength and much to think about. She must not move too quickly, ponder her decisions and plan where when and how to begin. Living with Paul and Melba was wonderful, nevertheless, when the time came and the house was finally in condition for her to move in she would do so. At least one of her questions had been answered. She could not sell her beautiful new home of happiness.

In the meantime, she needed an income in order to pay for the help needed. This brought about her decision to sell or lease the little house left to her by her mother and father. That money would get her started. She would pray and ask that they come to her with guidance.

One thing was definite; she would open an account at the bank, empty her grandfather's safe deposit box, rent one of her own and lock her grandfather's letter in it. Only she should could set eyes on it. She folded it, looked around and smiled. "Yes grandpa," she said, "I will take care. I will listen and wait for your signals."

She closed the door, locked it and smiled. "I'll be back," she said, and drove to the end of the drive opened the gate, closed it and headed into town. Melba would be anxious to hear how she had done and, as she suspected, she was ready and waiting.

"You are home early, I didn't expect you until late this evening. I'll give Paul a call and let him know you have returned."

"No Melba, not yet. I'm going to take a quick shower, change clothes and rush on into town. I have some business to take care of. I may be gone until five. Earlier if possible, and by then I'll be ready for dinner." She rushed into the shower, changed, returned and gave Melba a kiss. "When I get back you can tell me about your day. I'll see you soon."

Melba was left standing with her mouth opened. "Make it as soon as possible because I have things to tell you."

At the bank Carol arranged to have her accounts in California transferred to the local bank. Then, with a little argument and proof of ownership, she was given her grandfather's safe deposit box. She then asked for one of her own and they questioned why she did not use her grandfather's? "I have my own account and I would like my own box. I am superstitious," she replied, and took both boxes into an enclosed room. The truth was she feared they might allow her cousin to look into his safe deposit box and she could not take the chance. She examined the contents of her grandfather's safe box very carefully and placed everything into hers, with the letter from her grandfather tucked safely beneath it all. As she suspected her grandfather had quit deeded all the property into her name. She found no other letters of advice, closed and locked her safe deposit box, called the attendant, locked hers away and returned her grandfathers to the bank and gave them the keys. "This will be no longer needed," she said, "you can rent it to someone else."

It was around four when she left the bank and as she got into her car she saw Chad coming out of his hotel. She quietly drove away without looking in his direction. Glancing in her rear view mirror, she grumbled to herself and wished he would leave. His presence was annoying.

Once again Melba was waiting to hear how her day went. "You are certainly a busy lady! Do you think you can force yourself to sit in the kitchen with me for awhile and catch me up on a few things?"

"Yes, if you have tea I would prefer that to coffee. I will tell you about my day after you have told me what is on your mind."

Chuckling to herself, Melba made a pot of tea and brought out a few cookies to have with it. "I'll just have a spot of tea with you and let you know about our phone. I thought you would never get home!" She poured their tea and began:

"The same thing happened today; the phone has been ringing off the hook. We are all, including Chad, invited to Roy McFarland's for dinner day after tomorrow. I wondered how he happened to know Chad, but I did not ask. They could have met at your grandfather's funeral. At any rate, he said he had run into Chad one day in the bank. Since it is not for me to accept without talking with you and Paul, I told him I would have you give him a call. In case you have never heard of Roy McFarland, he is a billionaire and has a mansion not too far from yours. He has a lovely daughter who Chad will be pleased to meet, if he has not already done so and if he accepts the invitation."

Looking amused, Carol replied, "I just saw Chad in town but I don't think he saw me. It seems to me, if this Roy McFarland has invited him they must be on a friendly basis. Interesting isn't it? I will not accept the invitation until Paul comes home and we have talked it over. I need his advice about many things. No matter what I decide to do with the estate, he will be the one representing me. I am so lucky to have Paul and you."

Melba reached out and touched Carol's hands. "I see what is happening with you and Paul and it makes me very happy. Paul has been in love with you most of his life and I know you love him. Neither of you are good at hiding your feelings and it sounds to me like you will never leave us again. I would love to be your mother-in-law."

"My perceptive, lady, I have made up my mind on many things. You can sit in on all our conversations and then I will need only to say things once. When do you expect him home?"

"Right now," a voice came from the door. "You mean to tell me that you two are sitting here having tea knowing full well a hungry man would be coming home?"

"You are not going to go hungry my boy. There's a pork roast in the oven, sweet potatoes, veggies and Lemon meringue pie. Get into some comfortable clothes and we will eat."

"Wonderful! But before we eat, I would like to have a couple of drinks. How about you Carol. You look like a lady with much on her mind and I think a drink would do you good."

"Where's our hug and our kiss? You come through the door like gangbusters and start right in. Melba, wait until he gives us a hug and kiss."

Paul grinned, "My pleasure!" He kissed Melba, "There you are my lovely mother," and turning to Carol he leaned over and gave her a kiss, "and there you are my lovely Carol, "I have waited years for that. Now the two of you get with it. Dump that tea and I'll meet you in the living room."

"Guess we had better do as the master commands," Melba returned. "Come on Carol, let's have a drink while waiting."

He returned looking like an around home guy and asked, "Carol, why are you dressed like a business woman. Where is that becoming pink thing you had on the other night?"

"Here" she replied, "have your drink, sit down and I will fill you and Melba in on my day." She took a big swallow of her Vodka Tonic and began:

"As intended I got Gertie and we went to the house to clean. Gertie was shaking in her shoes, so we started in the attic and found nothing but a beautiful old standing mirror.

Gertie stepped into the room, saw her reflection in the mirror and thought it was a ghost! She let out a scream and ran for the door:

'Miss Carol, I told you there's ghosts in this place!'

I grabbed her by the shirttail and dragged her back into the room and made her look at the mirror. When she saw it was her reflection she sat down on the stairs and laughed so hard she wet her pants! You should have seen her face! It scared the living day lights out of her but I think it rid of fear. I told her if we saw any real ghosts I would chase them out. She asked if that was possible and was I a witch? I must have turned into one while living in the city. Well, I think I have convinced her that I am not, and she has agreed to work for me in my magnificent old house.

I do love my grandfather's mansion, with all its echos of the past, its gentility, refinement and delicacies. Each room has its own character, the furnishings are elegant and I cannot find it in my heart to give it up. It is a big undertaking but I have decided to keep it and never sell."

There was no mistaking the expressions on their faces. "I can see you are both wondering how I can afford to keep it, and with reason! I have questioned myself. Nevertheless, I can and will find a way. I will either sell or lease the home I own in Van Nuys, California. It is small but in a very good neighborhood and it should sell for a very good price. Property in California is not cheap!"

Paul eyed her with amusement. She was more than he had expected. She was determined and had a head for business just like her grandfather. "You will need legal advice Carol. You must not jump into this headlong without thinking it over thoroughly. The mansion is only one thing for you to think about. The property is another. Do you really realize how much land you own? What will you do with it?"

She tilted her glass to his, "Of course I will need legal advice and that's why I have you!"

He grinned devilishly, "Are you trying to use me?"

"Yes! You know how devious I am. Is it possible?"

"Of course, it will give me a chance to be near you, plus, I love being needed. But now I must tell you about a little visit I had today from your cousin. Around noon he came to my office looking dapper with too much style for this little town. He asked if I would join him for a cocktail and lunch. Without question I accepted and we went to our finest restaurant, ordered drinks and sat where our conversation would not be overheard. Our waitress eyed him, flirted and took our orders. He returned her smile and then got right to the point.

He is quite overcome with his cousins

beauty and questions her ability to undertake the handling of her grandfather's estate. That his grandfather left his huge estate to someone with little or no business sense disappoints him. He is in hopes that since we are friends I will be able to sway you into releasing your grandfather's estate as it is too much for you to handle and you should sell. If you decide to do so, he would like to be the first to offer you a bid.

I asked what his interest was in it? Were he to buy it, what did he plan to do with it? He would not divulge his reasons and carefully moved away from giving me a direct answer.

A couple of martinis later, he loosened up. He has been talking with Roy McFarland, one of our city's most prominent and notable men, and feels sure McFarland will offer to buy it.

Chad is assuming that since your father was a mere tailor you are not well off and will sell it as quickly as possible and for whatever you can get. Therefore, his firm will be willing to offer you a lucrative amount that would provide you with a sizable lifetime income.

I, again, urged him to give me his reason for wanting it so badly. What were his plans? This is it: he has in mind some sort of housing project he feels would better our city."

"I knew it," Carol angrily replied, "I knew he was after something! He not only insults me and my father, he also insults the city fathers. What makes him think he could better this city?

That is exactly what his company does! They buy and sell property and develop cheap housing complexes. Well he is out of luck! I will never sell it to him, no matter how much money he offers! And, for his information, until I have taken care of the house the property will remain as is! I can do only one thing at a time and the land is going no place. I have hired Gertie to help me with the house and tomorrow I am interviewing male laborers. I will need two or three men to help with the heavy work."

"That is not going to be cheap! Are you sure you are prepared to tackle all this? Have you given thought as to how long it will take for you to do everything?"

"Yes. I am calculating anywhere from six months to a year. As I said, I am either going to sell or lease the home I own in Van Nuys. That will give me an income. I have a sizable account of my own and a few investments that bring me a little income each month and, God help me - I will manage!"

Melba finally found her voice."Interesting isn't it? Chad has talked with McFarland, and only today we have all, including Chad, been invited to have dinner at the McFarland's this coming Friday."

"Now that is curious," Paul mused, "and what do you two have to say about this? Are you for it?"

"I am," Carol firmly replied, "but it will be up to Melba or you to invite Chad. No doubt he probably knows about it and is waiting for us to invite him."

"I will be happy to pass this information on." Eyebrows raised, Paul replied, "Tomorrow I will call Chad, have lunch with him and tell him about the invitation. I will watch his face very closely to discern whether or not he is surprised. He and McFarland may be trying to cook up something. Yes, we must accept McFarland's invitation." He grinned and patted his belly. "Do you know what this means? For tonight business is closed and I am hungry and ready for the roast pork and sweet potatoes!"

They took their drinks and headed for the dining room. "I love all this excitement!" Melba exclaimed. "I can hardly wait for Friday to come!"

"I wonder which of the two will be the first to broach the subject?" In the back of Carol's mind was the letter tucked away at the bank in her safe deposit box. Her dear old grandfather was so wise and had warned her about both. She already knew which of the two would win as it had been foretold. Still, she was curious to know what they might be planning. With the two of them biding against each other it should not be difficult to follow her grandfather's wishes and make old McFarland pay a million-five hundred thousand or more. Perceptively, she began to smile and Paul noticed.

"What is going on in that pretty head of yours. I can almost see the wheels turning."

She smiled deceptively and replied, "You could never guess!" Giggling she reached for the glass of wine next to her plate. "Let us toast to my success." They raised their glasses and together said, "To Carol's success! May we never lose her!"

After dinner, Carol got up and began to help Melba clear the table and Melba objected, "No honey, you and Paul go outside and enjoy this beautiful evening? It's a lovely clear night."

They did as ordered and sat next to each other on the front porch swing.

"This is nice, I love being here with you and Melba. Look at that sky filled with stars, that's a good omen."

"Carol, I love you. You have no idea what is going on inside of me these days. I go to work and try to concentrate on my clients and their problems and all I can think about is you. When the day ends, I want to rush home because I know you are here."

"I'm afraid I am too much like you. Old habits are hard to break. Being here with you is like turning back the clock. I never stopped loving you. We were young and separated for a reason; we had to grow up and have a better understanding of life before we could have each other. Now this is our destiny."

"You are right, this is our destiny and we will be together forever. Now that you are here, I will not let you get away." He put his arm around her and pulled her close.

She trembled and put her head on his shoulder, "You will not need to force me. I want you to hold me and never let me go. When you touch me I feel warm and safe. I dread the thought of moving into grandpa's mansion without you. Imagine me sleeping there all by myself! No wonder granddaddy had his things brought down stairs. He must have been very lonely without grandma, yet, he found a way."

"Are you really going to move into that house all by yourself? Why, when you have us?"

"When the rooms are in livable condition, I should. You are right, it is big and spooky but I have my reasons."

"Aren't you afraid of your granddaddy's ghost?" Paul laughed. "You don't expect Gertie to move into the servants quarters do you?"

"I haven't given it a thought. I just think I should to be there to oversee the work. It is a magnificent three story house. Two side by side doors open into a large foyer with a beautiful chandelier. All the main rooms have chandeliers. The lower part of the house has a library, my grandfathers study, the kitchen, two small apartments that must have been used by the servants, main dining room, small dining room, sun breakfast room just off the kitchen, small living room, a large drawing room, rumpus room, cloak rooms and you name it. Working my way through, room to room, is a tremendous job. The small living room across from granddaddy's study, has a small fireplace, much smaller than the one in the drawing room, that one is huge! I have not yet been through every room in the house.

After grandma died, Gertie moved my

grandfather downstairs, into one of the servant's quarters. He was getting too old for the stairs.

There are two floors of bedroom suites, all have a fireplace. You may have noticed the double wide chimneys, at the top of the house, two on either side. In the eighteenth century, homes were heated with fireplaces.

The second floor was occupied by my grandfather and grandmother and their two sons. It is a glorious house. However, it is far too large for one person. Do you suppose, when I decide to take up residence, you and Melba can come and stay with me? I know she would love the big kitchen!"

"What is there to hold me back? I love you and if I have my way we will pick up right where we left off and we will get married. Then we can all move in together. Melba will feel like an aristocrat and she and Gertie will have a wonderful time in the kitchen!"

Carol pulled away from him."Are you serious? I know you love me and you know I love you, but we have changed! When you really get to know this changed person you may not like me."

"I not only like this changed person, I love her. Yes, we have changed. I am older and wiser, do you like me?" His arms tightened around her.

She caught her breath, "With your arms around me I can think of only one thing, you. You set me on fire and awaken my other need. Here I am with this inheritance hanging over me and my head is in a whirl. You must turn me loose and allow me to think. I love you and want you and if I had my way we would have been married yesterday. Things are moving so fast I can't think! My greedy cousin Chad is here wanting everything and he and McFarland may be joining forces. I need to be able to correlate my thoughts! How can I when I am in your arms? Right now I can think of nothing but you and my need for you. If McFarland is as powerful as you say and wants my land he will check on my finances, both he and Chad."

"Put away your fears, I am here for you. Don't worry about either of them because they will get nothing past me."

She pulled closer to him. "I have loved you forever. When you walked into the candy shop and stood beside me, I thought my heart would stop beating. I still have your photo and have kept it on my dresser all these years. Kiss me and you will know exactly how I feel."

He held her gently and whispered, "I love you and this time you know it is forever."

Melba stepped out on the porch. "Oh, am I interrupting something?"

"Yes you are," they both said, "but we'll get used to it. We are renewing a long overdue love. When we were younger no one realized we were truly in love."

"Wrong," Melba replied, "I knew!"

That night as they lie in their beds their thoughts were of each other, wanting. Carol tried to put her emotions aside and think only of the job ahead but her desire was interfering. If only she could tell him about the letter. He had not an inkling as to her reasons for keeping her grandfather's estate. Things were moving far too quickly and he might feel she should sell. She had to find a way to prove to him she was doing the right thing. Perhaps if he would come to the house one night and sit with her by the fire he, too, would be visited. If that happened, then and only then, she would be able to show him the letter. In the meantime, if anyone heard about it, as her grandfather had said, the courts would say he had not been in his right mind when he made out his trusts.

Tossing and turning she punched at her pillow and tried to sleep. She could still feel the way Paul's arms felt around her and sleep was impossible. How could she concentrate on the house and property when all she wanted at the moment was him? "Think, think," she told herself, "you must make him understand your financial situation. How else can he advise you?" She punched at her pillow again, rolled over, and told herself to sleep.

Down the hall from her and her struggles for sleep, Paul was in his room going through the same thing. Tomorrow he would ask Chad to join him for lunch and invite him to McFarland's for dinner Friday evening. Amused, he smiled at the thought of the upcoming dinner. Chad and McFarland were definitely up to something and believed they were dealing with an incompetent woman. Watching their awakening would be enjoyable. He rolled over, punched his pillow and tried to put away his thoughts of Carol.

The following day Carol was up early, had hotcakes and eggs for breakfast and left to meet Gertie and the men she hoped to hire. She found her and her two granddaughters waiting with three tall strong men, Gertie's son Luke and his sons. All were polite and thankful for the promise of work. Each told her how many children they had and how long they had been without work.

Luke the largest and oldest of the group, was graying at the temples and spoke with a deep velvet baritone voice. Jacob was tall, thin, young and bashful and had three children. Mark, Luke's look alike son had five children. All were polite and anxious to start their day. She filed their names in her ledger and explained their days would begin at nine and end at five, for five days a week. Each day they were to check in and write the time of their arrival on the chalkboard in the kitchen. She would be there to make sure it was done correctly. If she found that some were lazing on the job, that person would be let go. If they did their job well, she would pay them ten dollars an hour. If they did a full eight hours work per day they would be receiving eighty dollars a day.

Luke was the first to speak up, "Praise God," he said, "you are an angel sent to us from heaven. God will bless you for this Miss Carol, and you will not have to worry about us. We will work and do things your way."

She smiled, thanked him for the blessing and said, "Now all of you get together, ladies too, and follow me. Lets get started."

She checked off the names of Gertie's granddaughters in her ledger. Bess, the older of the two, was a widow with four children to care for and educate. Fiona, the youngest looked like a young Gertie with wide innocent eyes. She was unwed, very attractive and a bit empty headed.

"I want you ladies to follow Gertie's orders, she worked for my grandfather and she knows this old house like she knows the back of her hand."

Lunch boxes in hand, they all piled into Luke's truck and began to sing. "Hallelujah, it's a new day and Lord we on our way!"

Gertie got into the front seat of Carol's car. "Miss Carol, does you knows what you done fo us? God bless you! Jus listen to that joy! We all been livin on biscuits and beans. Some- time ain't nough to go round. Them men an them girls give to they chillun."

When they reached the house, she clocked them all in and said, "Gertie, take the ladies into the house, go upstairs and get them started. You know exactly what I want done. You can take Jacob with you. He can get a ladder out of the tool shed and start taking down the drapes. I want them down, folded and kept with the bed-spreads. Once folded, Jacob can take them down and load them into the back of my car. I'll drop them off at the cleaners.

"Luke, you and Mark follow me and we will walk around the yard and house and I will point out the things I want you to start with such as the steps, broken shutters, missing shingles and things like that. Once you have taken care of that, the house is to be painted. Later the trees will be pruned and the gardens taken care of. I want to see the roses in full bloom. Everything will need to be fertilized and shaped up. The lawns are in bad shape and must be mowed. If at any time Gertie calls on you to help with something in the house, you are to help her. I have made arrangements at the local hardware store and lumber yard to allow you to pick up whatever is needed. Get receipts for everything, sign them and bring the copies to me. Your work, for the time being, is all outside. Jacob will be helping the ladies on the inside, but when they no longer need him he will join you two. We have much work ahead of us. I pray we will get it done in six months or a year."

"Yes, mam!" Luke looked excited, "Come on boys let's get to work!" He and Mark began to sing and their voices blended and filled with joy as they headed for the shed.

"I'll want those shutters painted white Luke, so you can put that on your list for the store. The house is to be painted Indigo blue. You may not be able to get that exact color, but I can snip a piece of cloth off of the back of one of the drapes and they can match it at the paint shop."

"Yes Mam! We just need to have a look in this tool shed and see what's here. We may need nails and other things. I'll make a list and bring it to you before we head for the hardware store."

"Good, you will find me in the house with the ladies. When you need me head for the top floor."

As she entered the bedroom where they were working, Fiona was saying, "Grandma, I never knew people lived like this! Just look at all these beautiful curtains! It sure ain't like the flimsy stuff on our windows."

"We's lucky we's got windows," Gertie replied, "don't you go poor mouthin the way we lives. We eats, you has clothes on you back an most of all, we's got each other. We's together an we's got love. God says we is to earn our keep by the sweat of our brow, so let me see you sweat!"

Laughing Carol said, "Now you listen to your grandma, she knows because she has done a lot of that sweating!"

"An I'is gonna keep on sweatin long as I lives. I had me a good man! He died an lef me with Luke. My boy an my grand-babies is all I got an I proud of them." She turned to Carol, "Bess looks jus like her granddaddy an ever time I look at her, I see'd him. God jus took him too soon."

Carol looked at Fiona, so young and so pretty. "Fiona, I want you to get the linens out of the closets in each room and place them next to the drapes and bedspreads. Then I want Jacob to put them in the car with the drapes. We can't make up the rooms until all these things have been cleaned. And Bess, I want you to get any clothing you may find out of the closets and put them on the beds. If you find any kind of jewelry I want you to do the same with it. Once the drawers are cleaned, we will put fresh covering on the bottoms and close them. Everything must be dusted and polished. I think there is polish in the kitchen under the cabinets, so bring up all the furniture polish you find and also some dust cloths. We are going to find more things in the linen closets in the hallways. It may look clean to you, but it is not! It is old and musty. I may lose some of it while being cleaned, but I hope not.

A voice in the doorway and Luke said, "I have a list here for you. Look at it and if you agree with everything Mark and I will take the truck and head on into town. Maybe you can take a string off one of the drapes for me to match the color blue."Stammering, he asked, "Is the time it takes going and coming back to be deducted from our pay?"

"Not if you go straight in and do what is needed without taking any extra time!"

"Well, how about when we stop and eat lunch?"

"I won't dock you for that either, unless you take advantage and loaf around in order not to work."

"Miss Carol, we will never do that! And we will get into town, get the stuff and get back here as quick as we can. And we will eat our lunch on the way into town."

She laughed, "I know you will do a good job for me and I trust you. Now get going!" She looked after them and knew she was doing the right thing. Looking up at the sky she said, "Thank you God. You have given me a job I pray I can complete according to your rules."

The entire day was spent on the third floor rooms and Carol kept giving order, "Now Jacob, I want you to go down, look in the shed and find the tallest ladder you can find. Test it and make sure it is safe. Then I want you to get a bucket and begin to wash these windows."

Jacob looked out of one of the windows. "Miss Carol, I won't need a ladder. There is a ledge outside these windows for me to stand on. There's plenty of room for me and my buckets. But I will need rags!"

"You git down to the kitchen an fine some vinegar! Ain't been nobody livin here fo long time, so I knows they's vinegar in the kitchen. You gonna need plenty to wash the dirt off them windows! They be rags there too. An if you see'd polish, bring it."

"If not, Gertie," Carol said, "there are plenty of towels and things in these rooms and he can use some of them. We have plenty."

Down the stairs he went and returned in seconds with two buckets in hand and a jug of vinegar. "These folks sure liked vinegar!" He handed Gertie another bottle, "Is this furniture polish?" It was. He stepped out on the ledge, began to wash and sing and the girls sang along with him.

"Gertie," Carol asked, "do you all sing all the time?"

"When we's workin, we's happy an when we's happy we sings!" She began: "There is power, power everlasting power, in the blood of the Lamb!"

Carol got a rag filled it with furniture polish and began to polish and sing along with them: "There is power, power, everlasting power in the blood of the Lamb...."

"They's back!" Jacob called from outside the window, "and looks like they's got a load of stuff."

Carol stopped polishing and ran down the stairs to have a look. She found them taking things out of the truck and stacking them in the driveway. Luke handed her the bill and she checked it over to made sure it had been signed. "Did you have any trouble getting this?

"No mam, but they sure had a bunch of questions for me to answer. All those folks want to know what's going on out here; are you planning to live here or are you selling or what? I couldn't answer any of their questions. I just told them you hired us to work and we don't ask questions." He laughed, "That didn't make them very happy! And they sure checked out all the things we were buying, paint and so forth. I got us an extra long ladder. I found one in the shed, but we really need two." He looked up at Jacob. "I see Jacob is working. How is he doing? Has he given you any trouble?"

"None what ever Luke. Everyone is at work and they are all singing while they work. To tell you the truth, I have never been so happy! Where do you plan to start?"

"Well first we will put all this in the shed, then I think we'll start fixing the broken shutters, the screens, the steps and things like that. After we get all the broken stuff fixed, we will begin to paint. You said to paint the entire house with blue paint. Is that right? Look at it and see if it is the right color blue. Once we have done all that, we will paint the shutters, porch railing and trim white, just like you want."

She looked at the paint. "It's perfect, but I think you will need much more. This is a very big house and you have about enough blue paint for the top floor. You also need to check out the roof and make sure there are no shingles missing. We don't want to have any leaks!"

"Yes mam, I'll have Jacob check the roof before we start painting. He can go through the attic to get to the roof. All these old mansions have a place where you can get out on the roof. Jacob is our climber. When he has finished the windows he can check the roof."

She smiled and thanked him, looked at her watch and realized they had about two hours left for work. The bill in her hand was a big one. She began to calculate approximately how much money she would need to complete the job, realizing she had only just begun. She had in her account at the bank a little over three hundred thousand. If it took as much as a year to get the house in shape it would cost her all of that and more. This evening she would talk with Paul about it and ask him to help her decide whether to sell the other house or rent it. She had in her pocket book, a roll of cash. Her thinking was that their first day of work would be paid in cash as she was sure they all needed it. From that day forward, they would be paid at the end of each week.

As they talked a voice came from on top the roof. "Hey down there! I've danced all over this roof and I ain't found no missing or broken shingles!"

Luke grumbled, "I swear, God forgot to give that boy his wings. Okay Jacob, now get down from there and help the women."

Carol laughed, "We have a couple hours of this day left. At the end of the day I am going to pay you in cash and thereafter I will pay weekly."

"God bless you,"Luke replied, "my wife is going to be mighty happy to see a piece of meat on the table."

Carol trudged up the stairs and entered one of the rooms just as Jacob crawled back in. "You nearly scared the life out of me Jacob, dancing around on that roof. Have you finished with all the windows on this floor?"

"Yes mam, and while I was in the attic I cleaned those two little windows the ones grandma says she's sees the ghosts in. "We need to clean that attic, too. You want me to do that? It won't take long."

"Yes, and after you have done that I want you to go from room to room and collect all the drapes, bedspreads and linens and take them down to my car. Did you eat any lunch?"

"Yes mam! While I was outside doing the windows I opened my lunch box and ate my biscuits and jelly. I'm just fine. I guess the ladies did the same. One thing you don't have to worry about is us eating; my wife makes the best biscuits in the world! A little jelly or honey and you are in heaven!"

At five o'clock they all gathered outside. Carol locked the door, counted out their money and handed each eighty dollars in cash.

Luke's eyes filled with tears. "We all thank you! You don't know how much this means to us!"

"Yes, we thank you,"Mark said, as he looked at the money in his hand, "tonight my babies are going to have some extra biscuits, mashed potatoes and hamburger gravy! We are going to have a feast!"

Carol held back her tears. "Why not some pork chops?"

"I have too many mouths to feed. I have mine and five little homeless kids to take care of. Hamburger gravy and mashed potatoes will be a real treat for them. There is nothing better than a big plate of hamburger gravy, mashed potatoes and biscuits."

"You have taken in homeless children? Where have they come from? Where are their mothers and fathers?"

Luke spoke up. "No one knows, Miss Carol. They have been abandoned with no one to care for them except my boy Mark and his wife. They were left out on their own – perhaps by unwed youngsters. They are not all black, three are white and all are loved."

"That breaks my heart! There is no reason for a child born in this country to go hungry, white or black. Mark is a fine man. He will be blessed for taking in those abandoned children. I am so happy to see he did not allow color to stop him from caring."

"Miss Carol, you are a fine lady but we still have a lot of growing to do. Not everyone is like Mark. We are still in the south and things are better, but there are always diehards who cannot give up their old way of thinking. Yes, we can work wherever we can find a job. Black folks are not the only ones looking for work. There are plenty of white folks around here who need jobs. Lots of families have moved away to find work some place else. But we can't do that! We have our little shacks we live in and as long as we can feed our children they suits us just fine. We have a little garden with potatoes and we can manage as long as we have flour, beans, potatoes and water. The Lord takes care of us. Right when it seems like we have been forgotten, the good Lord does something for us. And it was the Lord that sent you to us."

"You have humbled me. I had no idea there were so many people out of work in this community. It looks like a thriving area. I am so thankful there are people like you, people with hearts. I am happy to be able to help. God bless you. I think you have a gold star waiting for you in heaven. You are not to worry. I am going to keep you working and you will be able to feed those children. Today you worked hard. Tomorrow is Friday, I will meet you here at nine and we will start again. Rest well."

Gertie sat in the front seat of Luke's truck and the rest piled on the back and began to sing, "Glory – Glory Hallelujah," waving their hands as they disappeared out of sight.

Carol looked back at the house. "I'll see you tomorrow and soon you are going to look like new."

It had been years since she had done so much hard physical work, and climbing the stairs had not been easy. She was tired and ready for a warm bath, clean clothes and a tall Vodka Tonic. In the morning she would rise early and drop everything off at the cleaners. She was anxious to see their reaction when she handed them all the expensive bedspreads drapes, and sheets with tatting on the edges. The town would be buzzing.

"There you are," Melba said and gave her a hug. "Looks like you have put in a hard day's labor!"

"I have and I am dirty and tired. I need a good stiff Vodka Tonic, a bath and some clean clothes. Even my hair is dirty. I'll just mix me a drink and take it with me. My bones are ready to soak in some nice warm water. What a day this has been! Climbing up and down three flights of stairs is not easy, my legs feel like they're going to drop off. It was fun and it has helped Gertie and her family."

"You poor dear! Well you do just that and then come down to the kitchen and we can chat awhile before Paul gets home."

Carol found a nice tall glass, filled it with ice, mixed her drink and took a sip. "Yep, that will do it," she said, and went into the bathroom slipped out of her clothes, turned on the water, eased her body into the tub and relaxed. Her thoughts traveled to the orphans Mark had taken in and she wondered why the authorities had not questioned and looked into it. Mark surely had a heart full of love. She must try to find a way to give them more help. She stuck her head under the faucet, wet her hair and poured on some shampoo, worked her fingers through her hair and let the water run through it until all the soap was out. It would have been easier in the shower but soaking in the tub felt better. She got out, dried off, shook her head and her hair fell into soft waves. A little spritz of Dolce perfume, her pink jump suit and she was ready to start over.

"There you are, sit yourself down and tell me all about your day. Did the bath make you feel better? You look nice and fresh!"

` "Melba, I would just like to sit here and relax with my drink and watch you work! This is my rest period and when Paul gets home I will only have to tell it once."

Melba placed a bowl of popcorn in front of her. "Here, you need something to go with that drink. Did you stop to eat today?"

"You know what? I forgot! Well it won't hurt me because you keep stuffing me with all that fattening stuff. I don't want to grow out of this jump suit. Now tell me, what's for dinner? I've just heard all about hamburger gravy and biscuits."

"Well that's good healthy food but I have a little something else planned for us tonight. And remember, tomorrow night we are dining with the rich folks!"

"How could I forget? Now tell me what are we having? I'm sure it will be better than the food at McFarland's. I hope they don't serve Haggis! I am not ready for the innards, lung, heart and liver of a sheep. Wonder if he raises sheep? I may have trouble with my digestive system."

"Oh Lord, I couldn't agree more. Well I've been preparing things all day. If you will notice the dining room table has been set for four. We are having our high-nosed guest again. Chad is joining us."

"No! Not again! When will I get a chance to talk with Paul? Damn! What are we having? I bet you have gone all out to put that highbrow in his place."

Melba handed her a sheet of paper, "This: We will start with a chilled shrimp cocktail and follow it with a small cup of onion soup topped with cheese. A mixed spinach tossed green salad with artichokes, asparagus, topped with several small cherry tomatoes and mixed with cranberry vinaigrette. Accompanying that we will have steamed asparagus, a small diced butter fried potato pancake and an entree of prime-center cut of lamb chops with home made mint jelly. For dessert we have Peach Melba slices and vanilla ice cream topped with chopped toasted almonds and raspberry sauce. For the 'piece de resistance' an after diner drink of spiced coffee flamed with Brandy. How does that sound? I also told Paul to pick up two bottles of the French, Chateau La Tourette Pauillac wine to go with the lamb."

"My word! You really are going to show Chad that country folks know how to serve gourmet food? He may have thought meatloaf was beneath him but I noticed he ate it and went back for more. One would expect better manners from one with all his cultural refinement."

"My dear, his cutting remark did not go unnoticed! Very uppity he is. Guess he was born with a silver spoon in his mouth!"

Paul came through the door, kissed Melba and looked at Carol, "You are beautiful, give me a kiss and tell me what you two are up to." He handed Melba the wine. "Here's the wine you ordered, bit expensive you know! But it is what you said you had to have for this gourmet dinner. You will knock Chad right out of his socks." Winking at Carol he continued, "When someone steps on her toes she is a tiger."

"I see that! I have just read the menu! It's

a bit much after working with people who have so little to be thankful for. I am already feeling guilty. I would like to feed Chad biscuits and hamburger gravy!"

"That doesn't sound bad to me! Paul exclaimed. "I love biscuits and gravy."

"I'm sorry Paul. I am just out of sorts because Chad is coming. I have so much to talk with you about and I had hoped for time to tell you and Melba about my day, but with royalty coming it will have to wait. Could you slip away from your office for awhile tomorrow and come out to the house. We really need to talk, and it will take a little time."

"That can be arranged. My secretary can change my appointments to another day. I have a beautiful new client named Carol Nelson and she is more important than the others." He gave her another kiss. "Chad will be here by seven. I thought he should come at eight, but my dear mother changed my mind." He reached for Carol's glass, "Here let me freshen this one up. You are agitated so I think you need a little extra to quiet your nerves. You must have had a hard day and this unexpected visit, again, with your cousin has made it worse."

"I did, but it was a glorious experience. I love Gertie and her family and you need to hear all about them. With so little time, it would be impossible for me to tell you all about my day. We worked very hard and in my car are things for me to take to the cleaners, which means I will leave early in the morning and drop everything off. As for Chad, I hope this doesn't become a habit!"

"Mom do you have time to come into the living room and join us before Chad arrives. We have twenty minutes and you probably need a drink."

"Yes I have time! Everything is prepared and ready to go. Do not forget, I am a gourmet cook!" She laughed.

He poured their drinks and made a toast: "Here's to the cook and my beautiful bride to be."

"What?" They both reacted at the same time."

"Don't look so shocked mom! You must have seen this coming. Now then, I haven't been down on my knees in years and if I try I might not be able to get up. I love you Carol and although this is a bit impromptu, I am pleading with you to accept my proposal. I should have asked years ago! It is long overdue. Will you marry me?"

"I think I need another drink! This has been an all round surprising day! You are such a devil! You have deliberately caught me off guard. Yes! You know I will!"

He picked her up, kissed her and put her down. "You will not be sorry, I promise! This has been burning a hole in my pocket. I should have done this first." He opened the ring box in his hand and a four carat blue white diamond engagement ring winked at her. He slipped it on her finger and kissed away the tears streaming down her face. Looking into her eyes, he said, "Now we have something to celebrate and without knowing mom has made us a gourmet dinner for the occasion,"

"I have been praying for this," Melba said, "but I did not expect it with all else that is going on. I couldn't be happier. Carol has always been like a daughter to me and now she really is." She raised her glass, "To a perfect couple, may your love last forever!"

Their twenty minutes went by quickly and Chad, in his usual expensive casual manner arrived. He greeted them and surveyed Carol's apparel, obviously noticing she was wearing the same thing as before. "You are still looking beautiful," he said, "fresh as the morning dew."

She flashed him a smile, "I think you must be talking about my perfume. It does have the fresh scent of flowers, plus, I just got out of a bath. I worked very hard today at the house! But as you said last night, let us not talk shop. I have something to celebrate tonight." She held up her hand and flashed the ring at him, "Paul has just asked me to marry him."

He tilted his glass to her, "Oh my, isn't this rather sudden? I knew you were long time friends but I didn't know you were lovers!"

She smiled and replied, "You surprise me with your obtuse observation! Nonetheless, our love began years ago and fate brought us back together! Our grandfather Nelson! If he had not bequeathed me the estate, I would still be in Van Nuys, California."

Melba could sense the sparks about to fly and suggested they all retire to the dining room and she would begin to serve. "I worked a little extra hard today knowing Paul was going to pop the question tonight," she lied.

"Wonderful," Chad replied, "and for this auspicious occasion what has our gourmet lady prepared? I feel sure it will not be meatloaf or fried chicken!"

Carol narrowed her eyes at him and spat, "I would expect a man with breading, education and social deportment to choose his words carefully and not toss around uncouth insulting remarks thinking they would go unnoticed."

Chad face changed colors, "Oh, I have been misunderstood. I do apologize! I did enjoy the meatloaf and I was simply trying to inject a little levity into this joyous occasion."

Paul jumped in to save the evening as he could see that Carol was ready to pounce on him again. "Tonight you are in for a special treat as mother has quite outdone herself for our special evening. I can assure you when we dine at McFarland's you will not find anything to compare with this."

The three went into the dining room and were seated while Melba began to serve. Carol continued to glare at Chad but sat tight lipped while trying to control her outrage. Melba served the shrimp cocktails, sat down and waited while Paul poured the wine.

Unscathed by Carol's outburst, Chad glanced at the bottle, noted the vintage and remarked, "This is a fine wine, I've had it served with Lamb."

"Really?" Paul mused, with a devilish glint in his eyes, "I had no idea! It was mother's choice." He raised his glass, "Tonight I am the happiest and luckiest man in the world. To my bride to be for whom I have waited half a lifetime."

She looked up at him with love filled eyes and thanked him, "Yes, and to my very dear old grandfather who has brought us together. He would be pleased. Let us have another toast to grandaddy."

The expression on Chad's face was worth a million to her. He raised his glass, "And may you share many years of happiness!" Jesting, he said, "This trip gets more eventful by the day!"

The dining began and after the shrimp Melba brought in the soup. "Oh, my dear," Chad exclaimed, "one of my favorites, French Onion Soup topped with Gruyere. Where ever did you learn to make this delightful dish? This is like dining at Antoine's in New Orleans, and just look at this salad. Magnifique!"

Melba rose from the table, stating she was sorry she had not hired Gertie to come and serve for her. "Excuse me, I will return in a moment." A few seconds later she returned and served each their lamb and vegetables with a tiny bowl of homemade mint jelly at the side of each plate.

Chad was surprised and delighted, while inwardly embarrassed for having made uncouth thoughtless remarks. When the Peach Melba was served followed by the spiced brandy coffee and flamed at the table, "Madame," he said, "vous etes un cuisinier gourmet fantastique!"

Melba smiled, "Is that a compliment?"

"Most definitely! I am quite sure you are right Paul, I doubt we will have a dinner such as this at McFarland's. I am looking forward to meeting his wife and daughter. I am told his daughter is beautiful, an equestrian and has a stable of fine horses."

"He does," Paul replied, "and she spends his money taking trips abroad. The wonder is he can loosen his purse strings long enough to allow it."

Carol could see Chad's interest mounting. His trip to the country was definitely more than he had expected. "I think she must be exactly the kind of woman you would like Chad. Perhaps we will be having more than one wedding."

"I hardly think so," he returned, "but it is intriguing. Thus far, this trip continues to bring surprises. First, I did not expect to find my cousin so beautiful. We came from good stock, n'est ce pas?' I would love to know a little about our great-great grandparents."

"There are pictures of them on the walls in the mansion. When you do your tour around the acreage, you can stop in one day and I will show you a few. I might add, dress down as we are in the process of cleaning. I would not want you to get paint on your finery."

He blushed, "I suppose I do overdress for this area. Habit, you know!" Unperturbed, he continued, "I will look for something that will befit the occasion. Something that will please you, dear cousin." He then looked at Melba, "May I have another cup of your Cafe Brulet Diablique?"

"Of course. Is that what's it's called? I call it spiced coffee!" She left and returned with the spiced brandied coffee and flamed it.

Chad continued to gaze, unscathed, at Carol and sipped his coffee. "Have you given any thought as to what you will do with the estate? You have inherited our grandfather's magnificent mansion, including hundreds of acres of land. What are your plans for it?"

"I have not yet decided. At the moment I am zeroing in on the house. I can only do one thing at a time and I am not ready to think about the land. It will be there when I am dead and gone. To date, I have not been around the entire acreage. Nevertheless, it is truly very large and in time something must be done with it. With faith, I will find the right solution. Tonight we are celebrating our engagement and I no longer wish to talk about our grandfather's bequest to me. Melba has made us this lovely dinner and it must not be spoiled with, as you put it, shop talk."

"I agree, well said." He turned to Melba, "Dear lady any time you feel inclined to invite me for dinner, please do not hesitate because you are one of the worlds finest cooks. We have entertained clients from all over the world and hired cooks and servants to serve, but I can in all honesty tell you that none of them could surpass your ability. Again, I thank you. It has been a surprising and enlightening evening. If I leave early please do not be offended as I have not adjusted to the change of climate and find myself in need of more sleep."

They all rose from the table and he gave Melba a little kiss and turned to Carol, "I want to congratulate and thank you and Paul for sharing this evening with me. I may see you at the house tomorrow and you can show me a few of the old photos and things. I was there during the funeral but had little time to look around."

"I will be there with my crew of workers. If you don't see me just ask and they will tell you on which floor I can be found."

He raised his eyebrows, turned away and bid them goodnight.

"Thank God, that's over," Melba said, "you two go into the living room and have your little talk while I go into the kitchen and put things away. I might even have a little more of that Cafe Brulet 'what ever' spiced coffee,"she giggled. "Magnifique n'est-ce-pas?"

Without argument, they went in and sat by the fire. "Another evening of fun with your cousin! It went well, don't you think?"

"If you say so," she replied and snuggled up close. "He is still trying. I definitely expect to see him show up at the house tomorrow. That means we will put your visit off. Hold me, kiss me and let us not think about him. Let me feel your arms around me. I want us to get married as soon as possible. Not a formal wedding, just us together as quickly as possible."

"I will make the arrangements."

When she dropped everything off at the cleaners there was much to-do over the antique spreads, draperies and linens. "These are quite old," the man behind the desk said, "we can make no promises, they may not hold up under the cleaning. But we can promise we will do our very best."

Charming him with her smile, she replied, "I have heard wonderful things about your work, plus, I found old bills in my grandfather's desk from this very cleaners. They were all marked excellent with his or my grandmother's signature. Needless to say, this is why I have brought them to you. I feel sure you will handle them with the utmost care. They are precious! I am hoping to restore the mansion inside and out to have it look just as it did when it was built, and as it did when my grandmother was alive. It is a beautiful historical landmark for this city and you all should be very proud of it." The proprietor assured her he would pay special attention to everything she had brought in. "You must be the lady we have been hearing about. My daughter believes she went to high school with you."

"She very well may have," Carol replied, "please tell her she is welcomed to come out to the house any day during the week and I will show her around. I am usually there working with my crew."

He thanked her and said he would pass her invitation on to his daughter and asked if she might care to join them for dinner one night.

"That is very kind of you. You will note the phone number I have given you is the home of Paul Savage. I am staying with them as the house is not yet ready for occupancy." She held up her hand and showed him the ring, "We are engaged."

"I know Paul and his mother very well. He is my lawyer and it appears he is very good at keeping a secret. Wait until my wife hears about this!"

Carol thanked him and asked that he call Paul when the things were ready for her to pick up."

"I will do that. If you prefer, I can have them delivered to you at the mansion."

"That would be wonderful! I can't thank you enough." She left smiling to herself. Without a doubt he most definitely would do his best to see that everything remained intact; Paul was his lawyer.

Her crew was ready and waiting when she arrived. "Today," Luke said,"we will repair everything that is broken, renew hinges, steps and things, and once we have done that we will begin to paint the house with the color blue you you have chosen. The shutters and all the trim and porch railing will be white. My fearless boy Jacob will do all the high work. Before we get started we all want to tell you about last night. It was one of the happiest nights of our lives. We had a feast and a big get-together in our front yard with joyful singing and praising the Lord. One night we hope you will come and join us."

"I would love to Luke! That is the nicest invitation I have ever had. When our job is finished we will do that. I can't do it now because my bones and muscles are so sore I can hardly move. The stairs in this house are about to kill me!" Luke grinned and she said, "Don't you laugh at me! I'll get used to it," she moaned. "Now, I have clocked you all in, so let's get to work."

"Yes Mam!" The singing began and the activity rolled. Carol took Gertie by the hand and said, "Come on. Today we only have one flight of stairs to climb."

"Yes mam, an I thanks the Lord fo that! Jus what is you fixin to do with this old place?"

"I have not yet decided. I have to talk with God and granddaddy's ghost before I can make up my mind."

"Don't you go scarin me agin with them ghosts! I ain't over scarin the devil out myself! Wish you see'd the way they's all laugh when I tole them bout my ghost! Everone is askin is you gonna sell this place. It too big for you!"

"I am not going to sell it. It is mine and I am going to keep it. I am going to get married and stay right here in Cutterville. Paul has asked me to marry him. If we have a family, this house may not be too big."

"Lordy! You's a fast worker!"

"No I am not, Gertie! This is an old love story. We went together when we were young. Life just managed to keep us apart until now. As for this house, I will tell you this Gertie, it is not going to be destroyed, not as long as I am alive! You and your family are going to work for me and Mark is going to keep feeding those babies. Now let's get busy. Where are we putting all the clothing and things out of the closets? I would like them all to be stacked up in one of the rooms on the bottom floor because I don't want to climb these stairs more than I have to. Once they are all together, I will give them away or let you give them to some of the needy people in your community. How does that sound?"

"It sound mighty nice but most is fancy stuff and old. You might could put it in one them museums!"

"Yes, I could do that. However, it is not all that old. I think some of the things could be useful to your friends and relatives. If not, I can store it in the basement or attic until I am able to find a place for it. I'll think about it. The wonder is why my grandmother did not sell some of these things in her yard sale! I'm sure the townspeople would have loved them!"

"Miss Carol you knows how womans is, they ain't gonna give up nothin pretty, even if they gits too fat!"

They both laughed and began doing all the same things they had done the day before.

"Tell Jacob he has windows to clean on

this floor and he will be carrying things down to my car again. Darn, I should have had the cleaners to pick them up?"

The sound of voices rose up from below and one voice reached out in warm mellow tones. "Who's voice is that Gertie, it's glorious!"

"That my boy Luke. You needs to hear him in church! Nobody praise the Lord like Luke singin, 'Ain't No Better Place Than Heaven.' You knows when he sing the Lord is listenin! When he die, he goin straight to heaven!"

"Gertie, do you always sing when you are working?"

"Yes Miss Carol. When we's workin, we's happy an singin make it easy. You jus try an see'd how good it make you feel even when you is gittin up them steps!"She laughed.

At eleven thirty Gertie the girls and Carol stopped and sat around the table in the kitchen. Melba had made a lunch for Carol, but Gertie insisted she try some of their beans and biscuits.

"Miss Carol," Fiona said,"Eat them beans! They'll give you energy, but don't bend over!"

"She right," Gertie agreed, "If you eat my beans they gonna blast you right up them steps!"

"In that case, I'm gonna eat them beans!" They all began to laugh, like one big happy family.

Around noon a Lincoln convertible rolled up and stopped in front of the house. Gertie was the first to notice, "Now lookie here, you got company. Look like big time!"

Carol rose from the table and looked out,

"Oh crap," she said, "it's my highfalutin cousin. He just can't wait! Ladies finish your lunch and get back to work while I show this dude around. He would come while I was enjoying my lunch!"

She stepped outside and walked around the porch to the front steps. "Got yourself some wheels I see. Is it a rental?"

"Yes, it's about the best I could find." He looked up at Jacob standing outside one of the windows. "Do you think he should he be doing that? Aren't you afraid he will fall and sue you?"

She laughed, "That's Jacob, he has wings so we don't worry about him. He is one of my angels. He also dances on the roof and he is well acquainted with all the ghosts in the attic. Come on in and I will give you a little tour. Of course you realize you are causing me to climb stairs. I was in hopes you would wait awhile longer, but now that you are here let's get to it. We will start on the third floor. The drapes and spreads have been removed for cleaning. The furniture has been polished and the windows have been washed. We have only just begun."

She opened the large entrance doors and he stepped in and stopped to look up at the chandelier. "Oh my, that is magnificent!

"Yes. It is one of many in the house. All must be brought down and carefully cleaned. Imagine how it will look once all the dust is removed."

"Follow me." She walked toward the circular stairway. "To my right is the study, and next to that is the drawing room."

Chad very carefully put his hand on the stair railing and followed. "Could we not just go through the lower rooms?"

"No. Now that you are here you will see it all, even the attic if you like. Gertie saw a ghost in it the first day we were here!"

"If you are trying to frighten me you are wasting your time! I do not believe in such nonsense!"

"Oh that's right, if you can't see it, it does not exist." When they reached the top floor she stopped and said, "A few more steps and we can look at the attic."

"No thank you, this is quite far enough. Let's have a look at some of these rooms. I was hoping to see pictures of our grand parents and great-great grandparents. Are there any in these rooms?"

"No, you won't see them on this floor. These were the guests bedrooms and quite elegant. However, the framed paintings in these rooms are valuable as they were painted by early American artist."

They entered one of the rooms, he looked around and touched the fourposter bed. "This is rosewood and it is beautiful! Look at this chest of drawers and dresser and armoire! They all are rosewood. Carol, you could sell this furniture and make a fortune!"

Ignoring his remark, she said, "These are all suites. Our grandparents made sure their guests had complete comfort. Each has a sitting room, private dressing room and adjoining bathrooms. I suspect families were given rooms side by side. The bathrooms are beautifully tiled, and please note the hardwood floors. All the carpets have been removed for cleaning. I have someone coming to clean the chaise lounges and chairs in the sitting rooms. The drapes and bedspreads are at the cleaners and I have been assured they will be handled with the utmost care. Things must be restored and preserved. This house is a historical land mark."

"You have taken on an extensive and very expensive project. Are you really in a position to afford all this restoration, plus the labor?"

"Have you got your sleuths investigating? I think if you have they should have learned I am not exactly a pauper. Assuredly, I do not have your kind of wealth. I am a working girl and have not been left millions. Nevertheless, I can and will restore this building just the way my grandfather would wish."

Standing directly in front of a painting of the house as it had been, he mused, "And you believe you know grandfather's wishes." As the words left his mouth, the picture behind him fell to the floor. Startled, he jumped away."

Carol reached down, picked it up and hung it back in place. "You have just been sent a message. Be careful with your thoughts. This is how it looked. I wonder what caused it to fall off the wall?"

"Nonsense, I must have leaned against it. Shall we move on?"

"Yes, of course... We will find the ladies

on the floor below. There, you will have a chance to see some of the draperies, bedspreads and a few carpets on the floors. I could have shown you the ones on this floor, but once they were cleaned they were rolled up and put away until the hardwood floors have been treated and the drapes and things returned. Come, we will have a look there."

Jacob saw them enter and shouted in to Carol, "Howdy Miss Carol, the windows are looking good ain't they? Pretty soon I'll be able to help Luke and Mark."

"Did you eat you lunch Jacob?"

"Yes mam! I have it right here next to my bucket. You know I can't do without my biscuits and jelly!" Jigging around on the ledge he continued, "Ain't it a beautiful day?"

The sound of voices rose up from below and Jacob began to sing, "Swing Low Sweet Chariot,"and the ladies joined in.

Carol turned to Chad, "Have you ever heard anything more beautiful? Just listen to that glorious velvet baritone voice coming up from below. They sing all the time and I sing with them. It makes me happy and makes me know why I am here and why God sent me. But of course since you have not been introduced, you don't believe in God. Come, let us go below and you can look at the pictures in the drawing room. No work has been done in it and everything is dusty. We will just wipe away the dust on the paintings."

"You really do not like me, do you Carol?

What is it about me that brings out your wrath?"He stopped her on the stairway, and asked, "Is it because I have inherited more than you?"

In an instant she felt sorry for him. He was totally out of touch with life. Money was the only God he knew. "I could lie and tell you that I am very fond of you, but I am not. My reason being, you are completely out of touch with the real things in life. You have not stopped to look around. Wealth does not bring happiness! It does not bring love. You are well educated, yet think and live in dollars and cents. There is life all around you that you do not see. Just listen to those magnificent voices of Gertie's family. They are not trained voices, they are God given. You hear that word and it means nothing to you! With all your education, you have not begun to learn. You do not know the meaning of the gift of life! If I seem angry with you it is because your mind has frozen and come to a stand still. You are missing out on all that is truly important. If I were to ask you 'what is the most important thing in life?' What would you say?"

She paused and watched as he mauled her question around in his head. "Never mind, Chad. I see you cannot find the answer. Therein lies the problem. The answer is very simple. The most important thing in life is love. Without love, we are empty.

I see you as a very proud man who is satisfied with his wealth and surrounds himself with all the superficial things money can buy. To me you are empty, giving nothing to your fellow man, a man who looks with disdain at those who have naught. You are asleep and one day will wake and ask yourself what's missing? The answer will be something you can't buy: Love.

We need to learn Chad. Reach out, love and share what we have with those who have nothing but biscuits, gravy, love and faith. We must grow and never stop learning. I learn something new everyday! Being here working with these people has taught me so much! I pray the day will come when you will learn the reason and meaning of life. Until that happens, you have nothing."

"Well my dear, right or wrong you are certainly honest with your opinions and I admire you for that. However, I cannot wholly agree with you. Why not give up this project and your crusade or whatever it is, sell and take the money and enjoy life? Take a trip around the world and see things. Just think of all you and Paul could do with the money."

She glared at him. "There it is! I can see talking to you is a waste of time! Follow me, this is the drawing room and these are the portraits of our ancestors. They were not wealthy! They were simple folks who worked hard and lived hard. They had large families to take care of before there were any modern conveniences. The world we live in would have confused them. Theirs was a simple way of life. If they were proud of their success, it was because they had earned it. They had not inherited it! We must respect our ancestors for their courage and thank them for everything we have today." She allowed him a brief glance at the portrait over the mantel and guided him down the hall and into the library. "Here in our grandfather's library filled with books that will tell you all about our ancestors and their trials. These books are very delicate. Some may need to be professionally restored. I have not begun to clean them. Once that is done you may come and sit in his library and read. Who knows, it may change your outlook on life."

"I would love to come here some night, sit in front of this fireplace and..."

"Yes, you were saying? You would love to sit here some night and... perhaps feel the past around you? Chad, you have already begun to feel it. It does no good to fight it because if there is a force in this room that wants to reach you, it will. Messages come to us in different ways and if you receive one, recognize it!"

"Well my dear cousin, I don't know what I was going to say, but I will say you are right about this house. It is a treasure and I wish you luck in your endeavors. Nevertheless, I still feel you should sell the property to me and I could put a housing project in that would better this community." Something fell down through the chimney and he jumped away as soot blew out onto his shoes and trousers.

Carol laughed, "I think you have just heard my answer and your time is up! I'll see you another day. I have work to do."

She ushered him to the door and he hastened to his car. She waved and smiled as he drove away. He'd had a close encounter and refused to admit he felt it. She began to sing and joined the ladies.

"That's some fancy goodlookin fellow," Finoa said.

"Looks mean nothing, Fiona. He's my cousin looking for something he can't have."

"What's he after?" Miss Carol.

Gertie agreed, "What he affa? Is he a kissin cousin? If he is, you is takin!"

"Not to worry ladies, he is not a kissing cousin and if he was he couldn't have me. I keep trying to like him but he annoys me. He is rich and spoiled and thinks money is the answer to everything."

"Well," Gertie exclaimed, "it don't hurt!"

"Sometimes it does Gertie. My mom used to say that money was the route of all evil. And in my cousins case, it is. Now start singing, we have plenty of work left for this day. Where's Jacob?"

"He out the window singin and dancin."

Carol stuck her head out and said, "What in the world are you doing Jacob? Stop dancing around out there. You scare me to death!"

"Miss Carol, I gotta fix these shutters so we can paint them. I'm okay, don't you worry, the Lord ain't gonna let me fall."

"Well as soon as you can, come on in here and start taking all these drapes and things down to my car, just like you did yesterday."

Awhile later, Jacob entered, sat his bucket down and said, "I'm here and I'll get this stuff right down and put it in the trunk of your car."

"That's just fine. It is nearly time to quit for today. You all have done a good job. I'm sorry my cousin pulled me away from you. I was not much help was I? I'll see you all again Monday. Everyone come on down to the yard. I'm going to pay you again today because it is the end of the week. I know you need it and maybe Mark will be able to give those babies some extra hamburger in the gravy."

They all followed her down the stairs and as she stepped out onto the porch she noticed the door hinges didn't squeak and the steps didn't creak. She gathered them around her, counted out their money and gave it to them.

"Bless you Miss Carol, there will be a party this Sunday. If you get a chance, come on down!"

"I just might do that Luke. What time is your party?"

"Right after church. This time the ladies will fry chicken and all the neighbors will bring things. We have a bunch of tables and benches in our front yard. When you see all that, you'll know which shanty is ours! There will be people all over the place and Reverend Johnson will be there to bless the food. And his wife and children will be with him. You might like to meet him."

"Yes, I think I would like to join you and bring Paul and Miss Melba. What time do you get out of church?"

"About eleven and if you are there by twelve you will see people bringing extra food." He got into the truck and the rest piled on and began to sing and wave as they disappeared out of sight.

On the way home she stopped by the cleaners. The proprietor saw her enter and greeted her with, "My goodness, we don't have your things ready yet!"

"I'm sure you don't," Carol replied, "can you send someone out to my car to bring things in? It's the same amount as before and must be handled with great care. My grandfather's house has three stories, plus the attic. Thankfully, there is nothing in the attic to clean. This will take care of the second floor. Once that's done we will begin on the lower floor which will be entirely different. I do not want you to rush. Take time and care with everything. The next time I have a load of things to bring in, I would like you have someone pick them up?"

"I surely will Miss Nelson. It will be my pleasure. Folks have been asking me what you are planning to do with the place and I haven't been able to give them a clue."

"Folks have also been asking me and I cannot give them an answer. For now, suffice to say, I am keeping it and renewing it and once done I will decide exactly what to do with it."

"They are also wondering about all that land."

"Yes, I have also been bombarded with

questions about the land. I have a couple of ideas but I am not ready to be quoted. When it happens, everyone will know. Now I must run as we have a dinner engagement tonight. Just give a call and let me know when the first load will be arriving at the house."

"Will do, and enjoy your evening with the McFarlands."

"Excuse me! How did you know we were dining with the McFarlands?"

"This is a small town and there are no secrets in it. Word travels fast. Between Millie at the telephone company, the barber shop and the beauty parlor, you can't keep a secret."

"Thank you, I will keep that in mind and make sure I don't do anything scandalous."

She greeted Melba with a smile. "You were right Melba, the town is buzzing. How is it the entire city knows with whom we are dining tonight? The man at the cleaners said, 'Enjoy yourself with the McFarlands'."

"That's easy to answer. My day has been spent answering the phone because everyone knows. Might be my fault, I went to the beauty parlor to have my hair done and talked too much while there. No harm done, it just makes them all happy to think they are the first to know about something new going on in town. Honestly, it is so funny! I really enjoy stirring them up! Now sit down honey and tell me about your day."

"I must get myself ready for this evening so I will make it short. I had a visit from Chad, and it was comical. I'll tell you about it later. I want you to thoroughly enjoy it. Tonight I must wear something very special, something that will show off my ring." She flashed her hand in front of Melba. I have a Blackwell cocktail dress with a bear back and long pearls with a diamond clip that should knock their eyeballs out. I want Paul to be proud of me. Plus, I want my cousin to know he is not the only one with style."

"Honey, you do not need anything special to knock their eyeballs out, you have already done that with your mother's charm and beauty. It makes me happy to know you will soon be a part of our family." She kissed Carol, and said, "Now get on with you. We dine at eight."

Carol showered, and pulled her blond tresses into a dignified swirl around the crown of her head, applied soft makeup and dropped her dress over her head. Her long strand of pearls was perfect; a diamond clip held them together at her throat and allowed the pearls to hang down her bare back. A pair of diamond earrings, her wrap with the red lining, black shoes and purse and her ensemble was complete. She smiled at herself in the mirror. "This should keep speed with the McFarland's beautiful daughter." A last minute spritz of perfume and she stepped into the hallway.

A long low whistle stopped her and she turned to see Paul looking handsome, wearing a Givenchy gun-meddle gray cocktail suit, white silk shirt with pointy collar, slim silk woven St. Laurent tie and Calfskin oxfords. "Wow! You are a knockout," he said.

"And you look absolutely dashing my husband to be, not at all like a country lawyer."

"I couldn't allow your cousin to outdo me could I? Now let's have a cocktail and see what dear mother will be wearing."

She met them at the bar wearing a dark green cocktail suit with white lace blouse. Pearl earring, a gold brooch with pearls clipped on her lapel and green matching shoes and purse. "Do you think I will fit in with the high and mighty?"

They all laughed, "Who are we trying to impress?" Carol asked. "I think we look good in our work clothes. However, I will admit it will give me great pleasure to see the expression on Chad's face when we enter. He was at the house today. Drove up in a Lincoln Continental, and dressed to the nines. The rest of us were in our work clothes. I had a bandana tied around my head and was wearing my blue jeans with the holes in the knees. Fiona, the youngest, and very pretty, wanted to know who he was and thought he was handsome. I try hard not to be nasty with him but he really does get under my skin, and he knows it! He is so out of touch with everything, plus, he inadvertently insulted us. He said he thought I should sell and to think about all Paul and I could do with the money. We could take a trip around the world! I had to bite my lip on that one. He is such a prig! Fiona was right, he is good looking. He looks like my daddy but the resemblance stops there!"

"Drink your drink and don't get yourself

all stirred up. You should walk through that door looking and acting like an angel. We all must pull our act together and give a stellar performance."

"Paul. You are as anxious as I to see what goes between McFarland and Chad."

They were greeted at the door by a butler who took their wraps and escorted them to the drawing room where Roy McFarland and wife Jessie awaited. Paul introduced them to Carol and said he felt sure they knew Melba, and they did. Jessie McFarland, a tiny little brunette with pointy features and steal blue eyes smiled and took Carol's hand, "You look just like your mother, stunningly beautiful!" She turned to her husband who obviously agreed.

Roy was a tall robust man with red hair and Carol mentally pictured him wearing kilts. "Come in my dear, I have just heard about your engagement to Paul."

"News surely travels fast doesn't it? We have waited far too long. Life took us away from one another and now my dear grandfather has brought us together. Bless his dear soul."

"Please," Jessie suggested, "everyone join me. We can sit by the fire and chat for awhile before dinner is served."

The couple sitting together near the fire turned as they approached the fireplace and Chad rose and held out his hand, "Carol, you are looking ravishingly beautiful. Let me introduce you to Miss Rose McFarland."

Rose, a delicate willowy beauty wearing emerald green, tilted her head and her long red hair fell to one shoulder. In a soft, silky, voice she said, "I have been hearing much about the lady who inherited the Nelson mansion. We are neighbors, how nice. Do you ride?"

Carol smiled, "I'm afraid not, and if I did I would hardly have time. I work everyday in the house with Gertie, the black lady who took care of my grandfather. I have employed her and her family. They are lovely people and I am thoroughly enjoying the work, much more than I would riding."

Paul felt it coming, she was ready for bear, so he spoke up. "Having Carol here with us has brought excitement into our lives. At the moment she is staying with us, but once the mansion is ship shape she intends to move in. I am surprised you and Carol did not meet in school."

Before she could reply, Chad eyed Carol disapprovingly and asked, "Really Carol! How could you possibly consider living in that huge place by yourself?"

Carefully holding her glass in a way to display her engagement ring. "As you should have guessed, I do not expect to be living alone. My future husband and Melba will take up residence with me. We are a family."

Roy could contain himself no longer. "I clearly understand why you love that old house, it it is filled with old world charm. However my dear, I would love to know exactly what your intentions are concerning the property."

"Well now, that's the big question isn't it? Chad is very interested in it and most everyone I have met has asked me the same thing. No one has given a thought to the fact that I may have plans for it which I do not wish to divulge. That property has been in the family for many years. It has not been cultivated, nothing has been done with it. My grandfather might have had plans for it, but we will never know, will we? Perhaps other business, age and the loss of his wife may have destroyed any plans he may have had. We corresponded but he never mentioned the land. Had he talked with me about it I might be able to give you an answer. Be that as it may, at the moment I have no intention of selling it to any one person or any two who may be thinking of making me a joint offer. I will first complete the restoration of the mansion and then I will turn my thoughts toward the land."

A voice from the doorway of the dining room announced, "Dinner is served."

Paul escorted both Carol and Melba to the dining room and breathed a sigh of relief. Both men had received a low blow. Carol had gone straight to point.

Roy was seated at the head of the table and Jessie to his right. Since there was an uneven number of guests, she did not sit at the opposite end of the table. Carol was seated next to Roy on his left across from Jessie. Paul was at Carol's left across from Chad with Rose to his right across from Melba, who was at Paul's left.

A delicate white wine was served and Roy lifted his glass to welcome their guests. "This table is adorned with four beautiful women, let us drink a toast to them. First, to my adoring wife Jessie who tolerates this Scotsman, my lovely Rose, and Carol and Melba who are joining us tonight for the first time and hopefully not the last." He cleared his throat and continued, "Since it is Pheasant season we will be having fresh young Pheasant for dinner? I hope you all will enjoy it!" They all drank and he sat and continued. "Cook has a very special way of cooking these birds, Spatchcocked Pheasant. You will find them delightfully browned, until crisp on the outside and the meat on the inside moist and tender."

To go with their wine, an appetizer of bacon wrapped water chestnuts and pecans was served with a light berry jelly, followed by a salad of fresh greens topped with crushed walnuts. When the entree arrived, each had a small beautifully cooked bird. The backs had been broken, split, placed flat on the grill and brazed with Cherry wine until crispy brown. Alongside each bird, the plate was dressed with three slices of lemon, parsley, watercress, fresh vegetables and a small bowl of green herb sauce. It was quiet a long festive dinner with waiters coming and going. A dessert of walnut brittle candied orange vanilla ice cream was served accompanied with Irish Coffee and followed by an expresso liqueur after dinner drink.

All the while Chad sat looking like the cat

that swallowed the canary and Carol wished she had been seated next to him in order to spill wine on his lap.

After dinner they returned to the drawing room and the conversation between Carol and McFarland resumed. "Young lady," McFarland said, "I can see you have inherited not only your grandfather's property but also his stubborn nature. You are right in thinking I would like to buy some of your land. I am not asking to buy the entire acreage, I would simply like to buy the acres that separates my house from yours. I will be willing to pay you anything within reason."

"Mister McFarland, I like you. I believe you are an honest man. I love your home and your adoring wife. You are a very lucky man. Since the property has been here for so many years, I must ask you why you did not talk with my grandfather about buying a piece of it? If you did, why did he not sell to you?"

"I believe if his wife had lived I would have been able to do business with him. But after she died, I could not get through to him. I did offer him a sizable amount for the land but he would not hear of it." From beneath his bushy eyebrows, he looked straight into her eyes. "They say we Scot's are difficult, but we are not the only ones."

"Mister McFarland, I appreciate your honesty, however I am not ready to make a decision. I suspect you have talked with my cousin. He is also anxious to have it. He has some sort of scheme in mind for a housing project and seems to think it would better the community."

"Well I don't see how that could interfere with the land I wish to buy! His business is building and mine is horses."

"Have you talked with him?"

"As a matter of fact I have! He would also like to buy some of my land but, like yourself, I do not like the idea of his housing project."

Chad joined them, "Excuse me but I could not help overhearing part of your conversation. Neither of you are thinking in business terms. You have given no thought to the advantages a new housing annex would bring to the city. It would proliferate and give people jobs."

"Yes Chad," Carol agreed, "it would give people temporary jobs, but once finished where would they find work? You are talking about carpenters and landscape artists. Where will their jobs be when your project is finished?"

"They would find work in new shopping areas, department stores, restaurants, and so forth. You must look to the future. It is called progress. The climate here is, for the most part, nearly perfect year round. You both should give me a chance to talk in-depth with you about this."

"Well Chad and mister McFarland, I will give both your offers much thought. Tonight we have enjoyed a beautiful dinner and I think we have talked enough about my property. You will both have to wait. Do not push. I cannot hurry. My thoughts at this very moment are on that tall dark handsome man talking with Jessie, Melba and Rose. I think we should join them, after which, we must leave because I have a hard day ahead of me. You have given me much to think about and I will."

She excused herself and joined Paul and the ladies. "Paul, Melba, I think it is time for us to leave. Rose, Jessie, meeting you has been a pleasure. I thank you for such a lovely dinner. Perhaps when I have finished with the house, you, Roy and Rose will join us for dinner. This has been a very pleasant evening but must be cut short because I am a working lady and need my rest. Sunday, we are invited to a party in the black neighborhood. After church, Gertie and her family are having a gathering at their home. Everyone will bring food, rather like a pot-luck dinner. I am looking forward to it because they sing. And one of Gertie's sons has a glorious God given voice."

"Oh, how I would love to join in on such a gathering. It has been many years since I have heard their voices. When Roy and I first came here, we had a group of employees who sang while they worked. Since then things have changed and I hear very little singing. Perhaps when you have opened your new home, they will sing for us."

Carol gave Jessie a kiss, "They would love to sing for you. I intend to keep them on for as long as I live." She looked at Paul, "That is if Paul will allow."

Paul smiled, "I hardly think anyone can

keep this lady from doing what she wishes. I am looking forward to the future, whatever it may bring! Thank you for a lovely evening." He turned to Rose, "I see that you and Chad have hit it off rather well. I hope your friendship blossoms."

She smiled charmingly, "Only the future can tell. I am quite a traveler and I may soon be leaving on another trip to Spain. I do love Spain! The terrain is much like ours, plus the horses are magnificent. I am going there to buy and bring home an Andalusian.

Chad joined them, and addressed Paul, "I will take my leave as you do. Jessie, this has been a very pleasant evening and Rose, I hope we can get together soon. I will take you up on your invitation to go riding. How does Sunday sound?"

"Wonderful," she returned.

Jessie and Roy saw them to the door and Jessie took Carol's hand, "You are lovely, I hope we will see more of you."

"We are neighbors and I will definitely be seeing you. Again, I thank you for the lovely dinner. Goodnight."

As they drove home Melba said, "I would love to know how that Pheasant was cooked. It was delicious and I am usually not a fan of wild birds."

Paul laughed, "If I know you mom, you will learn. I think the evening went very well although I missed much of the conversation that passed between Carol, Roy and Chad."

"I will fill you in on everything but not tonight. If you are not working tomorrow we can go out to the house and spend some time in grandpa's study, and I'll discuss all my plans with you."

"If you do that," Melba offered,"I will make you a picnic lunch. With luck you will have a nice clear sun shiny day."

"Would you like to go with us and have a look around the place. I bet you haven't been there in years."

"Stop" Paul said, "I have an appointment tomorrow right here in town. I think we will forget about the mansion tomorrow. When I am through with the couple I'm seeing, I can come home and mom you can fix us a plain old country dinner while Carol and I sit on the front porch and talk. How does that sound?"

"Sounds like beef stew tomorrow night!"

Next day, wearing her blue jeans and blouse tied at the waist, Carol drove out to the house. This was the first time she had been in it alone since finding her grandfather's note. She eased the door open and went directly into his sitting room and settled back in his chair. "Well, grandpa," she said, "McFarland and Chad are dying to get their hands on your property. Some of the things Chad has said sound plausible but you said I should not listen to him and so I am not. McFarland is a likable man and polite but you have forewarned me about his tight fist.

This house is my first priority. I want to see it looking the way it did before grandma left. She loved fine things and I am trying my best to keep them in tact and looking as they did when this home was built in the eighteenth century. I know that grandma changed all the drapes and things, nevertheless, there is still much to do! Plus, I have questions for you about the land. Ten thousand acres is allot to think about. I have given it much thought. What should I do with it? I do not want to see it crowded with cheap housing."

As quick as a flash a group of small blinking stars came toward her and buzzed around her head like a nest of bees. She smiled, "Oh don't worry, I am not going to allow Chad to do anything like that. I'm in a quandary about how to start and what to do?

There are families here who need work and if I can find the right thing to do with the land I could put them to work and help them. What would you think about me cultivating the land with rotating crops of wheat, corn, alfalfa and sweet potatoes, peanuts or whatever? I don't know where to start but I feel sure there is someone in these parts who could help me with it. I believe the grass can be plowed under to use as a cover crop to feed the soil. What do you think?" She waited for a sign:

Appearing and moving slowly toward her from the corner of the room came a group of tiny lights amidst a veil. It luffed to and fro and looked as if it were going to take form, then turned as if dancing. "Should I take that as an approval?" The little lights danced up and down around her. "Well then I will talk this over with Paul." She held up her hand, "I am engaged to Paul Savage. I'm sure you know him, he is a fine man."

The clock on the wall chimed and two little figures danced out and around and back into the clock. "You are all with me, so with your approval I will continue on. But do not go away, I think you gave Chad a little scare the other day, although he will never admit it. I told him these walls would make him a believer. He say's he believes in only that which he can see. Poor boy is missing out on life.

When we dined with McFarland, he seemed to be taken with Rose, McFarland's daughter. I believe she is as spoiled as your grandson and they would make a perfect match! A sound like laughter filled the room and she knew she had been heard. "I wish you would do that for Chad!" Again, the sound filled the room. She leaned her head back and closed her eyes. "I love my new home and feel your love." An hour later she awoke, looked at her watch and said, "Oh my goodness, I've got to run! Paul and Melba will worry. I'll see you Monday." She locked the door and walked away smiling.

That evening while waiting for dinner, she and Paul sat on the front porch swing. "I think we should get a couple of these for the house. Also, we need to give the house a name.

What do you think we should call it?"

Paul thought for awhile, "Well that's a little difficult. Maybe since you are so happy with it, we should call it something like 'Happy Land.' How does that sound?"

"I think it needs something stately. What do you think of "Blue Manor?"

"Agreed, we will have a sign made to hang above the entrance gates. Those are big gates! We will need some iron work done in order to extend it. I can see it now, "Blue Manor" with blue birds holding it up. Do you think it would please your grandpa and grandma?"

"Oh yes and I love the blue birds!"

"It's settled. Now tell me what is it you need so badly to talk with me about?"

"My house in California. I must go to Van Nuys, get everything out of it that I want to keep and find a real estate agent. I have decided to put the house up for sale, furnished, as is. I should get no less than nine hundred thousand as it is in an excellent neighborhood, not highly trafficked, has beautiful landscaping and has been kept in tip-top shape. California property is expensive and I might be able to get more. I can ask for more and take less if necessary. If I keep it I will have to continue paying the taxes and the upkeep. If I were to lease or rent it, I would then have liability insurance to pay and still have all the taxes and so forth to take care of. What are your thoughts on this?"

"My thoughts are the sooner it is done the better. We can leave Melba with Blue Manor. She knows Gertie and she will follow your wishes and see that they do the same. When I see your Van Nuys home I will know better what to tell you. We can hire a moving company with a large van and bring back everything you wish to keep. A good agent should have it sold in no time. And, my beautiful lady, Monday we will get our marriage license and be married before we take the trip."

She threw her arms around him and kissed him. "This will be our honeymoon!"

"Now what else is it you wish to tell me?"

"Grandfather's land! I know I could sell it for a great deal of money but I don't think that is what my grandfather would want. If he had wanted it sold he would have left it to Chad. Therefore, I am mulling this idea around in my mind. Now don't laugh when I tell you."

He listened quietly as she explained her ideas about planting and growing crops on the land and marveled at her knowledge and desire to help all those in need.

"You are a marvel! Never would I have thought my little freckled faced gal would grow into such an intelligent, giving and loving person. I love you and I'm with you all the way. Go for it! There is money in wheat, corn, sweet potatoes, peanuts and other crops. You will need an expert to help you and, as it happens, we have an expert agriculturalist right here in town and he is none other than, Kenneth Dobbs."

She burst out laughing, "You are kidding! That is wonderful! In case you have forgotten, he was the first one to take me a prom. He was such an awkward fellow. What is he like now?"

"He is single, and still awkward but he is smart and just the person for you. He knows this soil and the weather and can get every thing done right for you. He can also tell you how much laborers get in the fields. Plus, he will get all the heavy equipment needed. Wait until Chad hears your decision! He is going to be livid!"

She wanted to tell him about the letter but could not. He had to be officially accepted by her grandfather's ghost before she could tell him.

Melba opened the door and looked out, "Okay you two, dinner is served. Beef Stew, sourdough bread, a green salad, ice cream and plain old coffee. We're not dining at the Ritz tonight!"

Paul gave her a kiss, "Good! I'm getting a little tired of all that gourmet stuff! Don't feel like dressing for dinner anyway!"

"Don't forget," Carol said, "we have been invited to Gertie's tomorrow right after church. Everyone is bringing something. It's a pot luck, with fried chicken and God only knows what all! Got to have the chicken because the Reverend and his wife will be there. And you are going to hear singing like none you have ever heard, better than the opera!"

"We can't go without taking something," Melba said. "I'll make a huge potato salad. What time will we get there?"

"Around noon, and we are not to dress

up. We will go in our everyday clothes. It's going to be a fun day and a new experience for all."

"What about church? Maybe we should go early and go to their church,"Melba replied, "do you think that would be acceptable? I remember going by it in the past and hearing singing. It's that little Baptist Church on the hill!"

"That is a wonderful idea! We should be there around nine. I imagine that's when their service starts. If it starts earlier, they won't mind if we come in late." Paul was a little hesitant but Carol insisted. "They will be thrilled to have us. I know them. I work with them everyday. Maybe we should get there around eight thirty and we could talk with Gertie or Luke before we enter." She won and they would do it her way.

The next morning they were up early and on their way. Melba had burned the night oil preparing a huge potato salad and had it in a large ice bucket. "I also made some lemonade, if the grownups don't want it the kids will. And I also stuck a couple of my pies in."

"Melba you are a wonder! How did I get so lucky? I've got a handsome blue eyed fiance and will soon have the best mother-in-law in the world!"

Luke and Gertie saw them arrive. As they got out of the car Luke came toward them with his hand outstretched, "Miss Carol, look at you! What an honor this is! Look around, everyone is staring because you are the first white folks to come to our church. It won't take mom long to tell them who you are. Let me introduce you to Reverend Johnson and his wife."

He escorted them up to the door where the reverend was standing greeting folks as they entered. "Revered and Misses Johnson, I want you to meet this lady, Carol Nelson, her fiance, Paul Savage and his mother, Miss Melba. They are wonderful folks and Miss Carol is the reason we are able to have our gathering at the house today."

The Reverend reached for Carol's hand, "I have been hearing wonderful Godly things about you. God bless you and welcome to our little church. There will be singing and rejoicing today! Now you just come right in and go right up to the front of the church." They followed him in and were seated in front of the pulpit. When the congregation was seated, he began:

"Brothers and Sisters – Praise be to God!" he shouted.

"Hallelujah! Amen!" The congregation echoed.

He continued:"We are gathered here today to praise our Lord and thank him for all our many blessings! "Hallelujah! Praise be to God! Amen! We want to thank the Lord for Miss Carol, who is bringing happiness to some of our folks, putting food on their tables and feeding all their children!"

"Hallelujah! Yes Lord! Lord! Thanks be to God!" The congregation chanted

He continued: "I can see it now! There is going to be a brighter tomorrow for us all because I know that the Lord has sent us an angel to show us the way! We has had some hard times! We have won some battles but we ain't there yet! We are going to the heavenly land. Now let us sing!"

Their voices began to rise: "Oh Lord – Lord - I'm on my way - I'm on my way to the Heavenly Land," and Luke's voice rose above all the others, " Oh Lord - it's a long long way - But I'll be there to shake your hand!"

Fiona's soprano voice lifted and joined in with the congregation's as chills and tears of joy filled Carol's eyes. Paul reached for her hand and held it in his and Melba took a handkerchief from her purse and dabbed the tears away from her eyes. The singing and preaching lasted for an hour and when it ended everyone was happy.

Carol, Paul and Melba rose and followed the congregation to the door, shaking hands and being stopped by many who wished to welcome and thank them for coming.

Once outside, Luke came to them, "Now you just follow me and I'll show you the way to our shanty. Ain't much to look at but it's home!"

People rushed in from every direction carrying food and drinks. Melba's ice bucket was placed on a table and Gertie helped her empty it.

"Miss Melba, "Gertie asked, "Does you members me? I see'd you lots at the old house when Carol's mom and daddy come to see'd her grandpa. They was wonderful folk! God blessed them with Miss Carol. Her daddy was a good man, nothin like his brother. Other day we see'd his brother's chile. Look like Carol's daddy! But he a high nosed somebody!"

Melba laughed and put her arms around Gertie, "Of course I remember you and I am so happy you and your family are helping Carol with that big old house."

"Is she tole you bout my ghost?" Gertie began to laugh. "I most scared myself to death!"

"Yes she did! And she has also told me about the wonderful job you all are doing. She comes home smiling and singing everyday. You are a blessing! Not just because you are helping her but because you have become family."

Children were running around in the yard playing games and now and then stopped at the tables to look at the food. Among them were a few little white children and Gertie noticed the expression on Melba's face.

"Yes mam, we's got white chillun here too. They chillun nobody want. Mark, is taken them an loves them like they's his'un."

"I don't understand why they are here? It seems to me the authorities should put them into an orphanage, or find some white families to take them."

"Maybe," Gertie replied, "but ain't no one come lookin for em an they's been here a long time! They's happy, an they's loved! They cain't git more love with white folk than they gits with Mark. They loves him! Sides, ain't no orphan place round here. You wants them taken off to a city where they's got nobody? Miss Melba, they's better off right here with Mark an his wife an babies. He got them chillun an five of his'un. They gits plenty to eat an plenty love. He taken in black babies too. Yard chillun with no folks."

"Well Gertie, I think Mark is a wonderful man and I thank God there are men like him. Now let me help you with the rest of this food. I need to talk with some of these other ladies. Everything looks delicious. I have never seen so much joy!"

The Reverend arrived and called all the people together and began: "Lord this is a beautiful day and a beautiful gathering with beautiful food, let's eat!"

Carol and Paul sat on a bench beside him and he began to ask question about the land Carol had inherited. Paul didn't want her to say but knew there would be no stopping her. She immediately began to tell him her plans for the land. "Let's just say I hope to farm it and maybe I will be able to put a few people to work. No one should go hungry in our country and no one should be without work, white or black. We are all God's children and we all have a right to this earth God has loaned us for awhile."

"Praise the Lord," the reverend replied. "You have just said it! All this earth belongs to God, and it is up to us to take care of it and make it productive for his children. We are all his children. Child, how did you get so smart?"

"I am not smart, Reverend. I have been blessed with this land my grandpa left me and I plan to do that which I think he would want. My grandfather was a good and loving man. He spoiled his wife and gave her everything she wanted, but she was a very dear loving and giving woman. I have returned to their home, where I spent many days as a child. It is a blessing from my grandfather and God. There is much work to be done and it is not going to happen overnight. It is going to take time and with the help of God, it will be done."

"Praise the Lord! Bless you child! I know it will be done! Now then, you have made this a glorious day! Let us enjoy this fried chicken the ladies have so graciously brought." His wife filled his plate with everything and they all dug in.

Paul put his arms around Carol, "What else am I going to learn?"

She shook her head, "One day at a time dear. I know I won't be able to employ as many as I would like because so much must be done with machinery. Today pickers are not needed in mass the way they once were, so I am thinking sweet potatoes and yams might be the answer. Sweet potatoes have to be planted and dug. I don't want to plant my fields with things that are going to be harvested with nothing but machinery. I want to see men on the ground working. I will have a talk with our friend and school mate, Kenneth Dobbs. And tomorrow, after we apply for our marriage license, I will return to work. Can we have a private marriage? One with you, me Melba and Father Sheehan?"

"What ever your little heart desires. I bet Reverend Johnson, would love to perform the service."

"Yes, that's a thought. I will talk with my ghosts about it. I know we would enjoy it but I am not too sure about my mother and father. I think they would want us to be married by Father Sheehan."

"Well I can tell you mom is definitely going to be thrilled. I noticed you did not say the blessing at McFarland's, and I noticed they also did not give it a thought."

"When I see others are not inclined, I am polite and mentally bless without their knowing. It would have been rude of me to inject my faith on them, although theirs may be the same. Perhaps not! We must not forget the battle between the Brits and the Scots over faith." She touched his hand, "What time should I be at the court house?"

"Nine, it won't take long. We'll be the only ones there. We will meet Father Sheehan in the church next door and tell mother to be there. After we've said our vows, you can rush off to work. I will arrange a meeting for you with Kenneth Dobbs. Better still we can have him to dinner, he and his mother."

"Oh my, what do you think Melba will think of that? She told me his mother had invited us to dinner. She might prefer that we go there."

"The web grows. We will ask, later. Let us enjoy this evening and be on our way."

"Reverend, we hate to see this glorious

enlightening evening end but, unfortunately, we must leave as Gertie and her family have work with me at nine tomorrow morning."

"I be there Miss Carol. Tha's to soon for me but I be there!" Gertie said.

"Luke came up and took her hand, "Yes, we will be there on time."

On the way home Paul told Melba about the need to have Kenneth Dobbs and his mother for dinner.

"I don't think so! No! That would be impolite because she has already asked for us to join them. I will give Eunice a call and let her know we will be happy to accept her invitation and I will find out when and what time she would like us to be there."

It was planned for Wednesday, informal, wearing every day togs.

Kenneth was overwhelmed at the sight of Carol. "You have been the talk of the town. I keep hearing about you. Paul tells me you are going to farm the land and will need my advice. Did I ever expect a thing like this to happen? No I did not."

"Nor did I Kenneth! I am a bit afraid of this new venture but feel I must do it. Just imagine, you are the one in the know who will help me! How lucky can I be? Can we sit in the living room and talk while your mom and Melba get things going?"

"You bet! Come on you two. You can tell I am not accustomed to entertaining. Would you like a drink? I don't have much in the house except a little wine. Mother doesn't believe in drinking."

"A glass of wine would be nice," Paul replied, "and I think Carol would like the same."

Kenneth got the wine and sat next to Carol, "Now tell me what you have in mind. She began with the acreage of the property and why she wanted to farm it."

"That is a big piece of land. Let me think. You are right in thinking sweet potatoes, but first I must say this. With that much property I think you should divide it and plant several different things. Lets say you split it in four parts, sweet potatoes, corn, peanuts, kale, broccoli or alfalfa. When one crop ends, you plow what is left under for fertilizer and the following season switch fields. The sweet potatoes can be comfortably planted for a year or so in the same field and later be moved to another where different crops have been. Rotating your fields will help keep the earth fertile and healthy. You will need machinery to dig the ditches and you will need people to control the irrigation and so forth. I can help you with all of that. I am sure you will have no trouble finding people to employ as there are many folks who are in need of work. Sweet potatoes can be planted by machine but I do not recommend it. You will have better luck having them planted by hand. Starter plants are put into the soil. Carol, you will be using a great many people and it is going to be costly. If the weather is good to us and your crops do well, it will be worth it to you and all those you hire."

"Tell me when we should start. Will we have time for a little trip to California?"

"Yes. While you are away, I will look at the land and begin to plan for you and get the ground ready. There is much to do. You plant around the last of Spring. But the starters come from small sweets that are kept in hotbeds until they have slips to plant. This will take about six weeks before you will have slips to plant. I should get those hotbeds going now. I can do that while you are on your trip. It is a year round process. Sweet potatoes and jams are delicate, bruise easily and once they have been dug they must be carefully placed into boxes and kept in a darkened area. Portuguese farmers often have cellars where they keep the sweet potatoes until ready to sell in the markets. There are yams and the original yellow sweet potatoes. Yams are what most people like, but they are not really sweet potatoes. You don't need to know all this. I will be most happy to help you and direct you. I will enjoy it! It has been years since I have done any real work. Most of the time I sit in my office and tell other people what to do, what they have done right and what they have done wrong. Do you have a building where the potatoes can be kept after the digging? If not, I suggest you get one built. Either that or you will have to lease from someone in town."

"I can have one built at the back of the yard, or there are several little cabins that were used for servants, maybe one of those would work. I am excited and can hardly wait to get started. What about the hotbeds?"

"When I look at the property, with your permission I can get that started now. I will choose a piece of land outside the wall, near the mansion for the hotbeds. That will be the easiest access to it. If you can, I would like you to place some funds for me to use into an account at the bank. Tomorrow, I will call Paul and tell him how much I will need to get started and he can arrange things at the bank."

"You are a gift from heaven Kenneth. How fortunate I am to have such a friend!"

"I am happy to do it Carol, and I am happy that you and Paul have found each other, again. He was determined to have you and he has won. I wish you luck and many years of happiness. Have you set the date?"

"Soon," Paul replied., "very soon."

A voice from the kitchen, "Everyone go into the dining room, time for dinner."

A week later they were husband and wife and Paul moved into Carol's room and Carol would whisper, "Be quiet," because there was no shyness in Paul's eagerness. Yet, he held her tenderly until his burning desire unleashed and she, in complete abandonment, melted into him as they became one.

"How can I tell you" she whispered, "about the nights I have lain awake thinking of you. The years could not take you from me. Hold me and never let me go."

"I will never let you go. I have waited half my life for you. Now we are one and here is where you will remain. Just having you out of my sight during the day is almost more than I can bear. Couples come in wanting a divorce while here I am beginning life. It is difficult for me to see their problems when I am so happy. I look forward to days end when I will feel you next to me and know it is real. I love you so much Carol, and I worry that you take on too much. You cannot save the world."

"No, I cannot. I am not God, but I can help a few. One evening you and I must go to the house and sit awhile. I want you to feel the warmth and love left there by my grandfather and grandmother. We can build a fire in the fireplace, watch the flames and talk. If you feel close to me now, you will feel even closer there."

He laughed and pulled her naked body up against his, "I doubt I could feel much closer than this."

"I'm not talking about physical closeness and you know it!"

"Yes I know what you are talking about but right now I feel close to you in all ways. Don't work too hard tomorrow, I want you to save a little energy for me."

"Fool," she replied, "I can never run out of energy for you."

The next morning they kissed and went in opposite directions, with Paul's promise to meet her at the mansion after work. Knowing their plans, Melba filled a basket with food and wine and told Carol to take it with her. "I know you are going to need this."

Gertie was full of excitement, "Miss Carol, Is you gonna hang round this house affa we goes home? This place has ghosts! Other night I see'd them ghosts floatin round upstairs!"

"Now Gertie, you know there are no ghosts in this house. We have been having a full moon and when the tree limbs blow around with the moon reflecting against the windows, it makes it look as if there is something in the house. But there is not, Gertie."

"I knows what I see'd! An they's ghosts!"

"Well Gertie, this evening my husband and I are planning to sit by the fireplace and talk. So if you see lights flashing around you will know who it is."

"You ain't fixin ta ask me t'live here with ya, is ya? Because if you is, I ain't!"

"There now stop fretting and let's get to work. Today we are working on the main floor. I want the small living room clean and shining because that's where Paul and I will be tonight, right in front of the fireplace."

"Is you spen-un the night?"

"No, I just want him to get the feel of the house. I want him to enjoy its history and me."

"I hopes nothin touch him!" She laughed, "It sure gived your cousin a start. He say he ain't believe nothin, but I see'd him git in his car right fast!" They both laughed,

The living room was cleaned and the

windows opened allowing in the scent of lilacs and honeysuckle. "Jacob," Carol called. "Gertie where is that boy?"

Gertie went outside and looked up. "Jacob, Miss Carol need you."

With one hand inside the window frame he leaned halfway out and paint brush in his hand painted one of the shutters. "Yes mam, I just have to give this one last lick and I'll be in." He leaned a little farther out, screwed his body around, finished the bottom of the shutter and climbed back in.

"That boy a caution!" Gertie said shaking her head. "He ain't got no wings but he think he do. When he meet his maker them wings gonna be there."

A few minutes later he entered the living room, "I'm here! Now what can I do for you ladies?"

"Go out and bring in some firewood and kindling and stack it in the box over there. I'm going to need a fire."

"Why? Are you fixin to spend the night here?"

"Shut your smart mouth boy and git that wood! You don't posed to asked no questions. Miss Carol don't works fo you, you works fo her. Now git on with you."

He grinned and danced out of the room. "I will be right back!"

"Gertie don't be so hard on the boy. He is full of life and happiness, although I must admit he scares the life out of me at times. I suppose when they start pruning the trees he will be up on the highest limb with his saw."

"Yes'm he will but the good Lord protects that boy. He ain't afraid, an he ain't gonna fall."

He returned shortly with an armload of fire wood and kindling. "You want me to start a fire for you. You got the windows opened and it is a mite cool in here."

"Not yet, but before everyone leaves for the night you can come in and get a good strong fire going for me and we will close the windows. My new husband is coming out to sit with me for a spell tonight!"

"Your new husband! Grandma didn't tell us you got married!"

"The man you saw me with in church, is the man I married. I have been in love with him for a very long time and now we are man and wife. We had been apart long enough and decided we had better get started."

Jacob was suddenly serious. "I think that is wonderful. Every man needs a woman and every woman needs a man. I couldn't do without my woman and my children. God has been good to me!"

Gertie looked surprised, "Jacob, I ain't never heared you talk like that. You always laughin an actin up! Miss Carol, look like you done made a change in this boy."

"You know I love my wife and my babies grandma. I like laughing and I like singing, but before Miss Carol gave us a job things were looking bad. Libby was crying and worrying all the time. Now she is happy because she knows we will have food on the table for our babies."

"I ain't never see'd Libby cry! An I ain't never see'd you act like no man afor. Luke done a good job bringin up his younguns. I'is proud!" Jacob laughed and put his arms around Gertie,

"Grandma, I love you. You are tough and you like to give orders, but there is coming a time when you will need to slow down and when that happens, daddy, Mark and me will take care of you."

Gertie began to cry, "Now you done made me cry. I ain't ready to give up yet. Long as these ole legs'll carry me, I'is gonna work. Tha's what the good book say we is to do. You has your wife an babies an I see you all happy an makes me happy. I'is gonna live ninety more years."

Jacob laughed, "Yeah, you gonna be as old as Methuselah!"

Carol went out and looked up at the third floor. The blue paint and white shutters were perfect. When finished it would look just like the painting on the wall. She looked for Luke.

"Luke, you have done a great job!"

"Yes mam, it's looking good but you were right, we will need more paint. I have been noticing cars drive by on the main road and slow to look up at it. I think the folks in town must be taking turns driving by."

"We still have along way to go Luke. The wall around the yard is going to need some repair."

"Yes mam, it has some missing bricks. There is a section out back that is gone and will have to be replaced. I think you can buy the old bricks to match."

"I'm getting dizzy thinking about it Luke. I calculated six months to a year and it looks as if it will be that long or longer. There is enough to be done on this house and land to keep us working forever."

"Have you decided to do something with the land?"

"Yes Luke, I have but we can't think about that now. We can only do one thing at a time. Nevertheless, I want you to know that you will be seeing a man beginning to do something on the land. He may need your help and if he ask you to help, I want you to do it. His name is Kenneth. If Paul and I happen to be away when he starts, and if you can't help him, you can get someone you know who needs work to help. I am trusting in you Luke! If that happens, be sure the person you get is trustworthy and a good worker."

"Are you going away?"

"On a very short trip to the house I own in California. I am going there to get an agent and sell it. We will not be gone long. In the meantime, Paul's mother will come each day to help Gertie and the girls. If you need anything at all, you just go to her the same as you come to me."

"I will do that Miss Carol, and I will keep everyone working just like when you are here."

"Good! Now let us finish this day of work. I will not leave until the end of the week. I will give you your checks then. I don't expect to be gone more than a week. I may be back the end of the following week. If not, I will give your money to Miss Melba and she will pay you."

"You don't have to worry Miss Carol, if we have to wait a week we won't mind. Pretty soon, if you want you can start giving us our pay at the end of the month. We know we have a job with you and now my wife hides a little each week. She is as happy now as she was the day I married her. No more worries, just happy and singing around the house like a young girl."

"That makes me feel good. Now go to work Luke so that I and Gertie can do a few things before the sun goes down."

It was after five when everyone piled into Luke's truck and headed for home. He and Mark had bought more paint and the second story was now blue and the shutters white.

They left the gate as Paul entered and she waited on the front porch for him. He looked up and grinned, "This place has taken on a new face. It looks grand Carol and, I might add, so do you." He took the front steps three at a time and swept her into his arms. "Are you ready for me?"

"Always," she said, and took him inside. We are going into the small living room. There is a fire in the fireplace. Melba's ice bucket is opened and sitting on the floor. I lit some candles so we have that and the fire. We can sit on the rug in front of the fire and have the dinner Melba made for us."

"You have thought of everything haven't you? Sit right here beside me and let me put my arms around you. Your hair is like spun gold in this light and you are more beautiful than ever." He kissed her, drew her close and their bodies synchronized with the flames in the fireplace.

"We are shameless Paul, rolling around on the floor in front of this fire, but isn't it nice?"

"It's more than nice, much more than I could have ever dreamed. I love you with all my heart. I want you to believe me and know that however your decisions with this house and property work out, good or bad, you will never be without because you will always have me."

She straightened herself up and said, "I believe you, and you will always have me. Now, do you feel a little hungry?"

He opened the bottle of wine and poured them each a glass. "My hunger was for you and what more can I want? You fulfill all my needs. The food and wine are an added enjoyment, because I am with you, my wife."

"What a nice sound that is. I am having trouble realizing it is true." She leaned against him. "This is wonderful. This is the first time in days that I have completely relaxed, and why? Because I have been so wound up and worried about us, our marriage, this house and how to manage things. I have not allowed my brain to rest. I must get this house together and the land producing. Do you really think I can do it"

"My little angel, you can do anything you set your mind to. I have seen that mind of yours working day after day and not just for yourself, also for others. You will succeed and this valley will turn into a field of gold. With true love you can do anything."

Just then a log dropped in the fire and some little stars came down around Paul's face. He began to bush at them thinking they were sparks from the fire. When they would not go out and continued to encircle him he asked, "Carol what is this? Is it bugs? Can it be fireflies?"

She laughed, "Just let them dance around you and then say you love me and see what happens."

"Carol, you know I love you."

"Now say to all those little dancing stars around you, I love her – I honestly do! Then wait and see what happens."

He watched the stars dancing around his head and said, "Listen, whoever you are I love this woman with all my heart and soul. If you believe me can you kind of dance a little farther away from my face?"Like a group of children the stars left and Paul sat quietly beside Carol.

"Do you know what all this is Carol?"

"Yes, I do. It is my grandfather and gran-mother, my mother and my father. They have come to check you out and make sure you really love me. If you had been lying you would not have seen them. They live here with us and they always will. They are the love and happiness that remains in this house." She reached for her purse. "Could you hand me my purse? I have something to show you. I'm sure grandfather won't mine." He handed her the purse and she took the note from it. "I took this out of the safe yesterday. I could not show it to you until you were accepted. When you have read it you will understand." The little stars remained behind Carol's head and watched.

From his sitting place on the floor, he reached for one of the candles, closed their lunch box, and placed the candle on top it. Holding the note close to the candle he began to read. As Carol had done, he read it and then reread it to be sure he had not missed anything. "This is why you have been so determined and have known what to do. This is why you have been so angry with your cousin and holding back on giving answers. You little devil! I knew you were keeping something from me."

"I dared not say anything until now. My heart would have broken if you had not seen my loved ones. But you did and now you know the secret and the magic of this house. I have been given credit for too much; I have only been following directions. Dear Gertie is right; this house has ghosts, wonderful, beautiful ghosts."

In a flash the action in the room was alive with brightness and laughter.

"Am I hearing laughter or am I imagining it? I've only had one glass of wine!"

"You are hearing laughter and so am I. Now hold me in your arms and it will quiet and they will leave us alone to love one another."

"Are you sure?"

"Yes, look!" She pointed toward the hall as the stars disappeared out of sight. "How do you like living with my ghosts?"

"I love it! Can others see them?"

"Paul, I really don't know. I guess it will depend on how they feel about a person. I know that Chad was given a couple of warnings and refused to accept them as an encounter."

"How so?"

"Well he made a couple of remarks that my grandfather did not like. Once a picture fell and another time while standing in front of the fireplace, something fell down the chimney and soot went all over his clothes. He refused to take it as a warning. But I think it scared him because he could not get to his car fast enough."

They both began to laugh, "Come here, my little love. Let's have this nice lunch Melba made for us and then head in. We don't want mom to worry about us do we?"

As they got into the car to drive away, they looked back at the house and little lights twinkled in the windows. They both said, "Good night, we'll be back."

At the end of the week the lower part of the house had been painted and the men felt they would soon be ready to begin on the yard, the fence and the trees.

"I think," Carol said, "you should first find the bricks for the wall around the yard and finish that before starting with the trees and maybe get that completed before my return. At least you can get started on it. We have moved very quickly. How long has it been since we began work? The weeks have slipped away from me."

Luke answered, "I know it seems like only yesterday since we began, but we have been working four months. You said it should take us six months or a year; I think everything will be done sooner."

"Not so?" Carol replied. "Looking at it from the outside, one might think we are through, however, we are far from it. There is still much to be done. All the woodwork inside must be checked and polished. We must be sure the rails and steps on the stairways are solid and firm and the railings must be polished. The chandeliers must be taken down, the chimney's must be cleaned and, oh my, if I keep talking I'll get a head ache. We will just keep working until we know it is finished. I want that bell by the carriage house polished and you may need to put a new cord or rope or whatever on it in order for us to ring it. We never know when we may need it. We have not talked about the servants quarters. I have not even looked into those. I wonder if they were ever used? They surely must have been. I have seen the ones in the house because my granddaddy moved into one of the rooms. Come with me and let's have a look into the little cabins out back. We will go through the house and out the back door."

"Yes mam!" He followed her through the house and opened the back door. A little path led to three small little cottages a few feet away from the main house.

"I'm surprised Gertie hasn't been after me to look into these." She tried one of the doors and found it had no lock. They walked right in and looked around. "My goodness, just look at this. These must be what were called slaves quarters!"

Luke, grimmest at the word, slave. "Yes mam, I suppose that's what they were."

Each were very bare and plain with a small open fireplace and a cast-iron pot hanging securely on a rod over what had once been a fire. Against one wall was a double bed, and in front of the fireplace two rocking chairs. On the other side of the room, a kerosene lamp hung in a bracket on the wall behind a table with two chairs. On the hearth, by the fireplace sat a small pitcher in a wash basin and under the bed one could see a chamber pot. An open doorway led into another small room with a bed and wash stand with a wash basin on it. A rocking chair sat on a small hand made oval rug beside the bed.

"These are sad little cabins Luke, and they have no electricity. I wonder how long it has been since they were used and how many people occupied each? Granddaddy's log-books should tell all there is to know about these cabins and the people who occupied them."

"I think mama will be able to help you

with that, Miss Carol. Why don't you ask her?"

"I surely will. Now you have further work to do and so do I and the ladies. Some of this will have to wait until my return. In the meantime I will have the ladies come out and get these quilts and things off of the beds. They are no good so they, along with these old straw mattresses, will be destroyed. These old chairs, tables and things, we are going to keep. I want you to treat and stain the wood and get them back into useable condition. These wonderful old rocking chairs must be taken care of. These cabins have history and much to tell us."

Luke laughed, "I do believe you are right! if mama stayed in one, she will tell you stories! If she did, it had to be before I was born."

"I doubt that Luke. She must have stayed in the quarters near the kitchen. She surely must have been like one of the family. That's why she is afraid of the ghosts!"

"I have never heard her talk about living in the mansion. I was born right in that little shack of hers and brought up right there. I had two brothers before me who died in their infancy. Life was very hard for mama and my daddy. Your grandma and grandpa were good to them, but my father developed tuberculosis and died after I was born and mama was left to bring me up by herself. For as long as I can remember, she walked to and from work, sometimes carrying a basket of clothes she had washed and ironed. She loved your grandma and grandpa and I think she was their favorite.

They may have asked her to live at the house but if they did, she preferred to stay in the house where she and my father lived. Your grandpa and grandma had other servants and I don't know where they lived. Maybe they lived in these places, mama never mentioned these cabins. Could be that her mother and father worked for your great grandma and grandpa. I just can't say Miss Carol. They may have been slave labor, and maybe at one time these fields were worked by slaves. Mama knows it all."

"Luke, I'm sure the history and names of everyone are in the books in the library and one day I will read all about the legend that belongs to this mansion. It was built in the eighteen hundreds so it has many stories to tell. Stories that we will never completely know. But now it has a new beginning and a new history that will fill the pages of a new book. I still have much to learn about my grandpa and grandma's home. I can remember a few of the other ladies cleaning and working around, but I was young and didn't pay much attention. My parents never talked about life at the mansion, even though my daddy grew up here. They bought their own little cottage and that's where I grew up. As I drove into town I noticed it had been torn down and a grocery store is where our house had been. It made me sad to see but, no matter, I now have this giant to take care of."

"It is old Miss Carol, but it was built with strong wood that has last through many years and with you taking care of it, it will probably last another hundred years. It is on this hill and when it rains all the water runs down to the land below. Your grandfather blessed you and my family when he gave you this old house. We all have much to be thankful for."

"Amen to that Luke! You are right. It is a blessing to all of us! Now let us get to work."

"Yes man," He smiled and walked away.

The end of the week came and with orders for Melba to take over at the mansion, Paul and Carol boarded a flight to Los Angeles. Paul was excited and anxious to be alone with his wife. "This is really our honeymoon, isn't it? Our first time alone and I love it!"

They rented a car at the airport and Carol drove them to Van Nuys and pulled into her driveway. Paul looked around and exclaimed, "This is beautiful! Just look at this yard covered in ivy!" He opened her car door, asked for the house keys and then picked her up in his arms and carried her into the house, "This won't be yours for long but for now it belongs to us."

Her arms were around his neck and she laughed and kissed him, "The bedroom is that way."

He took her into the bedroom, dropped her on the bed and sat beside her. "Now then," he said, "I am going to make love to you and you can make all the noise you want."

"You silly goose," she replied, "get out of this bed and bring our things in. I want to show you the rest of the place. We need to check the lights and see if we have any hot water. I could use a bath."

"If you say so," he grumbled and turned on a light, "One thing accomplished! You see we have light! I will now get our things out of the car and bring them in." He returned quickly and dropped the suit cases on the floor. "Okay, lead on!" He followed her through the house and out the back door. "A swimming pool! You forgot to tell me you have a swimming pool!"

"You want to go for a skinny dip?"

He looked around at the walls, "Can we be seen?"

"Nope! It's completely private and the other houses are not near enough."

He began to drop his clothes and so did she."Oh the water is cold! The pool heater is no on!" She shivered, "Just what we needed! When we get out we can shower and head for the bed. Tonight we can order pizza delivered and enjoy our first night alone."

"Sounds great," he said and pulled her under the water.

They came up sputtering and holding each other. "I love you so much! Are you enjoying this? Maybe I should keep the house for a get away! What do you think?"

"It is like we are in another world! If you want to change your mind, it is yours to do with whatever you wish!"

"I have not changed my mind. Just wait until you hear the helicopters over head, and the sirens and car brakes and so forth, I think you will be happy to return to our other way of life."

They raced, dripping, from the pool and into the house. "Towels are in the bathroom grab one and let's get in the shower." Like a couple of kids they got into the shower and laughing, got out, dried off and holding each other fell into bed. When their bodies were spent, Paul got out of bed and ordered their pizza. "I guess, while we are waiting you can show me through the house."

She wrapped a robe around herself, and said, "Follow me."

Walking through the house he marveled at the décor and stopped to eye a piano. "You have a grand piano! A Steinway! Do you play?"

She sat down, smiled and began to play, Mozart's prelude in C-sharp minor. "Yes love, you forgot that music was my major. I have been teaching piano for many years. My students were turned over to someone else when I received the news of my inheritance. I will miss my students. This piano will go with us and perhaps one day I will teach again."

He sat next to her and put his arm around her, "You are amazing. You are a woman with many talents; your best is in making love to me."

She stopped playing and looked at him. "You fill my life with love. Maybe God intended this! Perhaps we were too young to have been together before this day and this hour. I loved you then but it was nothing compared to the depth of my love for you now." She continued to play softly, "I've had someone taking care of the house while I've been gone and everything is clean and neat. I will call her and tell her of my plans to sell. It will make her unhappy as her daughter is one of my students. She does her practicing on my piano. Now she will have to buy a piano. The child is very talented and may become a concert pianist. I could give her this piano but since my father gave it to me, my heart says I must keep it. It will look beautiful in the drawing room at home. How does that sound to you."

"At home, meaning the mansion, sounds strange to me. It will take a little doing on my part to become adjusted to living in our new home. But with your grandfather's acceptance, I will." He looked with concern into her eyes, "Tell me, will our ghosts be watching us make love?"

She laughed, "No of course not. Anyway, you didn't seem to worry about it before!"

The door bell chimed and pizza arrived.

"Now look in the fridge and you will find a nice wine, unless Melissa, the lady who has been taking care of the place, has had a few."

He went to the fridge and found a bottle of Lancer's Rose. "Perfect! Couldn't be better! Goes perfectly with pizza!"

"You probably would have preferred Bell Agio Chianti but that I don't have."

"My dear, a bottle of beer would suit me fine."

"Oh I didn't think of that. There may be some in the fridge."

He threw a couple of pillows on the floor by the coffee table, "Come here, open that box of Pizza and sit with me here on the floor. This is what I call happiness! We will eat this and go to bed and in the morning we will find a realtor.

She laughed, folded a piece of pizza and shoved it in his mouth. "How's that?"she asked, and had the same, saying, "Thank you God!"

"I think before we go to bed, we should call mom and let her know we have arrived and are safe. She is probably chomping at the bit. I will do that after our wine and pizza. She will understand."

An hour later he called: "Mom you would not believe this beautiful house Carol owns. I am surprised she wants to sell it! How is everything going with you and the workers?"

"You are not to worry, everything is fine. Gertie is a caution! We have fun remembering old times. The men never stop but ladies like to laze a little. How long do you think you will be out there?"

"If possible, we will get everything done within a week or two. First an agent and people to come in and clean for the sale. Then a hauling van to deliver the things Carol wishes to keep. The agent, realtor, will put a lock on the front door that only she can open. I'll take pictures of everything to bring and show you. Here's the number you can call if you need us. We love you and will see you soon."

He looked at Carol, "Everything is fine, she is having a ball and feeling necessary."

The following day they started and Carol had a party for her students who were very unhappy to see her leave.

The house went up for sale at 1,600,000 dollars.

They hired a van and packed Carol's piano and other treasures and, after saying a sad goodbye to her California home, they boarded a plane for Cutterville in less than two weeks.

On the plane Paul said, "I kind of hate to go back. I have enjoyed having my wife all to myself for nearly two weeks. It has been a fun filled honeymoon."

Melba was waiting with the news and could hardly wait to see all the photos. Their first night home was cocktails and catching up with things.

"Your cousin Chad has been calling, still anxious to talk with you. McFarland has called numerous times, seems he has seen some sort of action going on in the field close to the wall and is worried. He wanted to know if you had sold the land between his place and yours. Of course I said I didn't know. Kenneth has, also, been anxious for your return. He is the one McFarland has seen working. Kenneth has hired some of Luke's friends to help him with whatever he is doing and McFarland and Chad are dying to know what's going on."

"Wonderful! Tomorrow I will get into my work duds and get out there to see what the rumpus is about. Tonight I just want to relax and enjoy some of your home cooking. What have you got for us tonight?"

"I hope you like it. I wanted to fix something that would allow me time with you two before dinner, beef stroganoff, a kinpira-collage of veggies, a fruit salad and I thought you might enjoy some of that brandied coffee again. I love it and would really like to have it."

"Well mom," Paul said, "let's get at it! We are tired, hungry and anxious to hit the sack."

The next day Carol stopped and caught her breath as she looked up at the large sign above the gate. Extended on chains two blue birds held up a blue cut out cast-iron sign: Blue Manor. The house majestically towered on the hill above and smiled down on her. On either side of the drive well trimmed hedges led the way to the house.

Jacob, sitting on a mower waved to her as she passed by, "Morning Miss Carol, welcome home. Seems like you've been gone forever!"

She smiled and motioned for him to come to the house, and everyone inside dropped what they were doing to greet her.

Gertie was the first, "We's missed you Miss Carol. Ain't the same when you's gone."

She looked around, "And I have missed all of you. And just look at all the work you have done! Everything looks grand!"

Luke spoke up, "Yes mam, we wanted to surprise you and have the sign on the gate for your return. You would not believe the amount of people who have been driving by and asking questions. Some of them want to know if this is a Bed & Breakfast. And that Mister McFarland is wanting to know what's going on out there in the field. Look out there Miss Carol. See those workers? They are putting in something called hotbeds. Mister Dobbs hired them."

"Wonderful! I'm anxious to see Mister Dobbs and learn how much they are costing me. He is an expert, knows his business and has permission to hire and fire."

"He will probably show up around ten thirty. He gets right out there and works with the men and they like him. He asked me about those little cabins out back. Seems he has some idea about what do do with one of them. I couldn't help him with that, just told him what you had ordered us to do."

"Oh, I know what he has in mind. Now let me get back with Gertie and the girls?"

"Yes mam! Just look at them! They are anxious for you to see all they have done. They have been polishing and shinning everything."

As she walked through the door Gertie was right behind her, "Seem like you's gone forever. Is you gonna stay now?"

"Carol gave her a hug, "It felt the same to me. Now come with me into the drawing room. I am having some things brought here from my home in California and I want to decide where to put my piano."

"Does you play piano?"

"Yes Gertie, I do. Help me decide where

to put it. Have you done much cleaning in here."

"Not yet! We be gittin to it!"

"I see the drapes are down and look at this! These French doors open out onto a little brick patio next to the garden. This will be a perfect place for the piano."

Gertie, stood shaking her head, "I never knowed you play piano. You is somethin else!"

"I do Gertie, and I can't wait to hear you all singing along with me. We will have a big celebration just with you, your family and us on the night we have finished with everything. I forgot to ask Luke, has anyone shined up that bell?"

"They's doin it now. The men done taken it down an it in the kitchen. Fiona bout rubbed the skin off them hands polishin it. It shine like a new penny!"

"Let's go have a look."

Bess and Fiona let out a scream, "We have been trying so hard to get as much as we could done before you got back. You are looking awful happy! You and your new husband must have had a big old time! Bet you've been making whoopee!"

"Yes we did! It was like a honeymoon."

Gertie looked closely at Carol, "Is you got a bun in the over?"

"What?"

The girls began to laughed, "She means are you going to have a baby?"

"Gertie! My goodness! It's much to soon for that."

"Don't take long!" Gertie exclaimed.

"No, it doesn't and we worked at it. It was fun!"

The girls laughed, "Miss Carol, ain't you ashamed talking like that?"

"No I ain't ladies. I love my husband. But now I have to get my mind on work! Can't stop working, thinking about making love."

The ladies screamed with laughter and Gertie exclaimed, "It ain't never stop me!"

Carol could see that Gertie was slowing more and more each day and she didn't want to push her old tired bones. She allowed her to give orders to the girls and paid her the same as she paid them.

"Come on Gertie, the drawing room is waiting for us. Let's go do some dusting and thinking about how to rearrange things to make room for that piano."

"Mm-mm, you sho likes work!"

"It's for a good cause Gertie. This is our home and I want it to look like we belong here."

Over the fireplace, a life sized painting of her grandmother looked down on them. Sitting in her chair, wearing a lavender gown, hands gently folded in her lap, her portrait gave the room a feeling of peace. In front of the fireplace two hand crafted rosewood sofas upholstered with silk chenille floral designs blended with her lavender gown. Adding to the ambiance of the room, a large ornate bowl of bone china flowers sat centered on a hand carved rosewood coffee table between the two sofas.

They each looked up at the painting. "She was beautiful wasn't she?"

"Yes mam, an jus as pretty inside. I loved that lady. She was good to me." Tears fell from Gertie's eyes. "She act like I'is family. An them boys, your daddy an your uncle, stand round under foot in my kitchen when I'is makin pies. I taken trimins, rolled em, put cinnamon an sugar on em an bake em. You shoulda see'd them babies grab them things and run. Them was nice days Miss Carol. Nice days. When my two baby boys git the fever, your grandma gits a doctor an tries to save my chiles. I never had nothin but boys, an the onliest one that lived was Luke." Gertie's face washed in tears.

"Gertie, when I have a baby you can make some little cinnamon rolls for him. Dry your tears and get your dust rag and let's get started."

She began to sing a happy tune and Gertie joined her. "I'm Alabamy Bound - if that old train don't stop and - turn around!"

"That nice, Miss Carol, how you knows that song? My mammy were a slave in Alabamy. Now you done brung her back!"

"It's a happy tune Gertie! You want to sing something else?"

"No mam, it be nice to think bout my mammy. Now you is married, who is I to call you?"

"You can keep on calling me Miss Carol, Paul won't mind. Sometimes he calls me Miss

Carol."

"When he do that?"

"When we are making love Gertie!"

Gertie laughed, "Hum-mm, you bad!"

"Miss Carol," a voice from the kitchen called out loudly, "there's a man here to see you."

"I'll be back Gertie. Take your time and if you get tired, sit awhile." She left, went out to the front porch and found Kenneth waiting."I see you have the hotbeds started. Exactly what is it they are doing?"

"They are stacking them very carefully in rows and, after that, they will cover all the beds with a clear plastic and stake it down or fasten it within frames so that it will not blow away. The heat from the sun, and the warmth of the soil and fertilizer will make them sprout. The sprouts, or slips, are what we will plant."

"Sit here in one of these chairs by the table and I'll have the girls bring us some lemonade while you tell me more." She called out, "Bess can you bring us some lemonade and some cookies?"

"Yes mam, right away." A few minutes later a large pitcher of lemonade was on the table and two tall glasses and a platter of cookies. "I made these this morning because I knew you were coming home."

"Thank you Bess, they look grand." She poured Kenneth some lemonade and as Bess walked away, she said, "They are my family. Now tell me, how much am I paying the men an hour?"

"You are paying them seven dollars and fifty cents an hour. If they become long time laborers for you, they may work for a little less. Luke chose the men and said they were honest and steady workers. Thus far he is absolutely right."

"I heard you had company from a couple of other sources."

"Oh, you bet I have! McFarland is very anxious to know what is going on, says this is a part of the land he was hoping to buy from you. Of course I told him I knew nothing about it? He grumbled and left. I'm sure you will be hearing from him."

"I'm sure you are right. I know exactly which land he wants and here is what I would like you to do with it. Have you by any chance made up a map of my property?"

"Yes."

"Well let's have a look at it."

Kenneth pushed the pitcher of lemonade aside and unrolled a large piece of paper, spread it out on the table and began to point out acreage. Now, this is McFarland's house and this is the land between his house and yours."

"Kenneth, I can see that you are putting the hotbeds on the side of the hill next to my house, that must be because they will get the direct sunlight there, is that right?"

"Yes, they need the warmth of the sun. You are a smart lady."

"Just look at this map, directly below that

is a strip of land that is flat and I believe that's the part he wants. Most all of McFarland's land is mountainous. My great grandfather, who built this house was very smart and planned well. The house is on a hill and below it most of his land is flat. I imagine he grew cotton on it. I'll have to look that up. At any rate, what I would like to have you do, is plant the section of land McFarland wants, in alfalfa. Could we do that? "

"Yes, a very good idea. Look at this." He began to point out different sections of land and how he thought it should be planted. The best place for these potatoes will be on this extra large level piece of property and behind that is a foot hill that would be good for corn. But of course we can't do anything with the sweet potatoes for another six weeks, it will take that long for the sprouts to start. Once they are ready we will get them in the ground. I will have to hire more men then. I can begin, now, and seed the alfalfa with a machine. I should also get some corn and other things going."

"I am leaving it all up to you Kenneth. You know who to hire and what to do and I know nothing. So I am in your hands."

He smiled, "I wish! But Paul won that battle. You look like a very happy lady. You are very beautiful,"he said, looking at her adoringly. Then he blushed and sputtered, "How does Paul feel about moving into your grandfather's mansion?"

To ease his embarrassment she let his compliment slide by."If Paul were poor he might object, but Paul is not a poor man and is content to move in. When the time comes, we and his mother will live here. That, of course, is in the future. We are not yet close to it. I rather like things the way they are. I am happy to stay in our little home in town. Paul and Melba have been very content to live a simple life in the home she and her husband built. As you know we just got back from putting my home in Van Nuys up for sale. I am hoping it will sell quickly because it will help pay for all the workers and things."

"To be honest with you Carol, I had been wondering how you were managing to do all this. Your cousin Chad has been around asking me a few questions. He has hinted that he does not think you can afford any of this."

"He is wrong. We can manage, Paul and I. If I run short Paul will help me, but I do not expect to run short."

"Wonderful. I have been looking at those little buildings behind the big house. If you will allow we can board up one, weather proof it and use it for a storage room. We will need a place to store the potatoes after they are dug. If we find that one is not enough, can we use two? I don't expect to need that much room but if and when the time comes, can we?"

"Yes. I will turn one into a warehouse. If possible, I would like to keep the other two in case we need a place for workers to live. It's just a thought. Those cabins were slave quarters and they can be turned into very nice comfortable little houses."

"Good then it's settled. Shall I tell Luke what will be needed?"

"Yes. Anytime you need something go to Luke. He will come to me for an okay and then he will get on it."

"Settled, now I had better get busy. I can't believe I am working for you!"

"You have not told me how expensive you are."

Grinning, he replied "I will give my bill to Paul and let him shock you. I'll see you another day. I'm so glad you are back." He paused and stammered, "We all missed you."

She went back into the house and on into the drawing room where she found Gertie stretched out on one of the sofas, sound asleep. For awhile she sat in a chair across from her and just looked at her. It seemed Gertie had lost her fear of the ghosts in the house. Gertie opened her eyes. "Oh Lordy, you back! These days if I sits too long, I falls to sleep."

"That's perfectly alright Gertie. I'm glad the ghosts don't keep you awake!"

"Well I ain't see'd none! Has you been talkin at that Kenneth man, what he doin?"

"Gertie, I am planting the fields so that we can grow crops and put more people to work. What do you think of that?"

"Glory be to God! You's an angel sent down to us. These is happy days. Thanks be to God!"

"Okay get that dust cloth moving and

let's sing a little."

They began, "There is power – power - wonder working powers, in the blood of the lamb…" Voices came from the kitchen and joined in.

"Jus waits til the Reverend hear bout this! They gonna be singin and hallelujahin at church Sunday! Glory be to God!"

"Gertie you are such a joy! I don't think I could do this without you. You turn everything into happiness. I love you Gertie!"

"Long is I ain't see'd no ghosts! Not even mine, I'is happy!"

A surprise visit came from McFarland and the ladies in the other room called out in loud voices, "Miss Carol, you've got company!"

"Gertie, join the girls while I see what this man wants."

"I knows him Miss Carol. Bet he gonna fuss bout them men in the field."

"You may be right!" She walked with her into the kitchen, stepped out the door and walked around the porch to the front. "Mister McFarland, have you come to see what a wonderful job is being done on my home? Doesn't it look grand? Of course there is still much to be done but once it is finished it will be a treasure for this city to cherish. It will remain a landmark when I am dead and gone."

He smiled warmly and joined her on the porch.

"Please be seated in one of these chairs.

Can I have the ladies bring you something? I think we have some lemonade. It's kind of warm out and you might enjoy it."

"Yes, that would be nice but a mint julep would be better!"

She called for Fiona. "Yes Miss Carol, what can I do for you?"

"Do you know how to make a mint julep? If so, please bring two and a bowl of salted peanuts."

Fiona smiled at McFarland, "Yes man, Bess can make them." She returned with two tall mint juleps, a sprig of mint at the top and a large bowl of salted peanuts. "Would you like a pitcher of these?"

"Yes please, with lots of ice." She turned to Roy, "Gertie and her family are wonderful, and thoughtful, and so thankful to be earning a living." She sipped her drink, "Now then, tell me what brings you here."

"I've been watching all the work that has been going on and I compliment you. The house and yard look like a page out of history. Your grandfather let it run down after he lost your grandmother. I'm glad he left it to you. Had he left it to Chad, it might have been destroyed. I am here to ask what you are planning to do with the field? I see some sort of work going on near the edge of your wall."

"Yes. They are putting in sweet potato hotbeds. It is my hope to plant the fields and put more people to work. I have learned that this community has many people in need of work and I hope to help."

He cleared his throat, "Before you have planted all the fields I would like to make you an offer on the land between my estate and yours."

"Oh, I don't think so, Mister McFarland! I have already given Kenneth Dobbs orders to plant that area in Alfalfa."

"My dear, I am about to offer you much more than you can make off of a field of alfalfa."

"That is not the point, Mister McFarland! My wish is to put people to work."

"That is a very noble thought, however my dear, alfalfa once grown will just sit there until it is time to be harvested and that will not take many men. It can be done with a machine. Let me tell you what I am ready to offer."

"You may offer, but I doubt I will be interested."

"Just like your grandfather aren't you? Well how does five hundred thousand dollars sound to you."

"It sounds like a generous offer, but I'm sorry, I am not interested!"

"Young lady, do you really want to refuse that offer?"

"Yes, I really do!"

He took a big swallow of his drink and shoved a handful of peanuts into his mouth and leaned back in his chair. His cheeks matched the color of his red hair. Steadily staring into her eyes, he said, "What if I offer you seventy-five?"

She filled his glass, sipped her drink and smiled. "I still would not accept."

"What?" He stood up, marched around on the porch, looked toward the field, grumbled and returned to his chair, downed his drink and poured himself another. "Exactly what do I have to offer you in order to get that property?"

She laughed, "Let me see! How about one million five hundred thousand? I think I could let you have it for that!"

"Young lady, you are out of you mind!" He got up and stormed off of the porch, "I think you will see it my way when that alfalfa field does nothing for you!"

"That remains to be seen sir. Now you drive carefully, you've had a couple of drinks!" She could almost hear her grandfather laughing and saying, "That's the way to do it!"

That evening after dinner, while sitting on Melba's front porch, she told Paul about her visit from McFarland. He laughed, "According to your grandfather, he'll be back. I hope he's right because you have really turned down a bunch."

"I am not afraid honey. I know that my granddaddy knew what he was talking about. That old McFarland wants that land for his horses and with me planting alfalfa on it, he wants it even more. I suspect he has plans of putting a racetrack in out there in order to train some of those animals his daughter keeps buying."

"You are a little devil aren't you? What other plans do you have in your head."

"I'm not quite sure Paul. I know there is something else I must do but I haven't been able to figure it out. Maybe when we move into the mansion it will come to me."

"Knowing you, I am sure it will."

"Let's see what Melba is offering tonight and then we can go to bed. I expect that van to arrive tomorrow with all my things. That will mean having Luke, Mark and Jacob help with it. Also, I expect the drapes and things to be delivered. I am anxious to get everything back in place, the carpets down, the linens put away and most of all to have our rooms made up so that we three can move in."

"Sounds like we have a very busy week ahead of us. Will we have time for a little lovin? I need to hold my gal in my arms and make love to her."

"Yes, we will always have time for love despite all our other activities. Now kiss me and listen. We must tell Melba to give thought as to what she wishes to have moved out of this house and into the mansion. Can't wait to see her face when we tell her."

"Tell me what? Dinner is served!"

"What's for dinner?"

"Drop biscuit chicken pot pie, and a small green salad. Hope you like it. And for dessert, a chocolate fondue with a touch of whiskey, and fat marsh-mellows on skewers. You can have as many as you want to dip in hot chocolate, graham-cracker crumbs and whipped cream. Then, because I am so in love with the brandied coffee, we'll have that with the Marsh-mellows."

"Wonderful, I'll just get us a little light

wine from the bar while you ladies get seated."

He returned with their wine, poured it and gave a toast, "Here's to our future in Blue Manor, where you, mother, will live like an aristocrat and have a ball in the kitchen."

"What are you talking about?"

Carol answered, "Mother, we will soon be moving into the mansion, our new home. Paul and I made this decision and hope you agree."

"Do you mean you want me to move away from here and in with you?"

"Mom," Paul answered, "yes, we do! Don't you want to be with us? You will not just have a room, you will have a suite of rooms and you can take everything from here that you want. It will be your private little world."

"Oh, my!" Melba downed her glass of wine, "I never expected to live like the rich folks! What am I supposed to do with my house?"

"You can sell it or keep it and rent it, whatever you wish. It belongs to you!"

"I would like some more wine. I must think about this. It's too sudden for me to decide!" She giggled and sipped her wine, "I think I'll love living in a mansion! Can we eat chicken pot pie there?"

Carol laughed, "We can eat anything you like and if you need help, we will hire you some help. I'm sure Gertie would love to get into the kitchen with you and teach you how to cook some jambalaya, old fashioned collard greens and green beans with pork fat."

"I'm looking forward to it. What news

this is! I won't tell a soul until the day it happens. Oh my! The town will be on fire with the news. Now then, lets eat!"

"Mom, Gertie's jambalaya will never top this chicken pot pie."

Paul was in the barber shop when the moving van went by. One of the other men in the shop said, "Wow! Looks like someone is moving into town. Have you seen any signs of new people or new homes going up?"

"Your new neighbor has been here for quite some time. That's my wife's grand piano and some other things she wanted to keep. She is selling her home in Van Nuys, California and when the mansion is ready, we are moving into it."

Sam, the barber said, "I know James, would be happy to know it is going to be lived in. He loved his home and we all hated to see him go. He was a wonderful old friend to everyone. Now his granddaughter, your wife, has brought it back to life."

Fred, one of the other customers in the shop asked, "When it's finished are you going to have a grand-opening so that all us poor folks can see what it looks like?"

They all laughed and Paul returned, "If I know Carol very well, I'm sure she will! She is determined to keep up the old family tradition in every way possible."

"She sure has," Joe replied, "I have even seen people working in the fields. She's making allot of people happy, that's for sure!"

Kenneth Dobbs walked through the door. "If you need to find someone this is the place to look. I just saw a moving van go by, could it be heading out to Blue Manor? If so, I guess that's where I can find Carol."

"You're right! She left with the birds this morning and she is expecting to see you. Is there anything I can help you with?"

Kenneth handed him a piece of paper,

"Yes, you can add something to this."

Paul got out of the chair, paid Joe and said he would see him next time. "Let's go to my office Kenneth and I'll take care of this."

Kenneth placed a list of things on Paul's desk. This is a list of prices for all the machinery, and the hours of all the help we are using, plus, my bill and the amount of money I will need you to put into the working account on the house and land. Are you able to do that?"

"Matter of fact I can. This is a hundred thousand. Do you think that is going to cover everything?"

"I don't know the exact amount we will need. I just made it a round figure, it may take more or it may take less."

"Okay, I'll call Carol and tell her to transfer this amount into your working account at the bank. Have you anything left in it?"

"Yes, I've covered everything up to date, but I will soon be needing more. The machines are not cheap. Fortunately we don't need them full time. It might pay to just buy them. I don't know, for now leasing is fine."

"Are you happy with the way things are going?"

"Yes, the alfalfa field is already looking good, the corn takes awhile and I've planted peanuts. In another two weeks we will plant the sweet potatoes. I have a reverse-go-devil out there right now, making ditches and mounds for the sweet potato slips to be planted. Could be that a week from now those plants may be ready to put in the ground. They are looking good and she will make money with the sweets. And, by the time they are ready to be dug, the storage building will be ready."

"Hold it Kenneth! I know nothing about this farming stuff! That is for you and Carol."

Kenneth laughed, "Right! Can't expect a a lawyer to be interested in farming, can I? I'll go see your beautiful wife."

Paul watched him leave and thought, "Poor Kenneth is hopelessly in love with my wife."

Kenneth paused before entering through the gates of Blue Manor. "Nice name," he said out loud and moved on. He found Carol near the delivery van directing the men.

"Be careful with that piano, I don't want to find any scratches on it. Follow me and I'll show you right where it goes."

Kenneth got behind her and the men and followed them into the drawing room. Light was filtering in through the opened French doors and Kenneth stopped to admire the magnificence of his surroundings. The floors had been polished, the furniture cleaned the chandelier sparkled in the sun-light and the picture over the mantel completed the history of the room.

"Just put it over here and turn it this way so the light will come in to my left."

The men very carefully unfolded the legs of the piano and placed it exactly where she wanted it. She lifted the lid, sat down on the piano stool, ran the scales and began to play ever so softly, Moonlight Sonata. Her hair glistened in the sunlight and she smiled sweetly at Kenneth. "I'll be with you in a minute. I just had to see if the piano was still in tune. I'm afraid it is not. I hope there is someone in town who can tune it. Now let me finish with these men and then you and I can talk. Go into the kitchen and tell the girls to get you something, lemonade, coffee, cookies, sandwich, whatever you might like and when the men are through bringing things in we will all join you for a bite of lunch. I feel sure they will need a beer or sandwich or something before they leave. The ladies will be happy to take care of you. Just have a seat on the front porch and I'll be with you as quickly as possible."

Filled with the hopeless agony of love for the inviolable, he turned and left the room.

She had the men take the remainder of things up to the master suite, thanked them, tipped them and gave them a check for the moving.

"I thank you very much. If you would like a little lunch before you head for the city, you can join us on the front porch."

"We thank you mam, but we would rather stop along the way for a quick bite in the truck stop restaurants. Your home is like something out of the movies."

"Thank you, it was built by my great-great grandfather. I am blessed to have inherited it. I thank you, again, and have a safe trip home."

They left and she joined Kenneth for lunch. "Now tell me what's on your mind. I had a call from Paul asking me to transfer money and I have done so. What else can I do for you?"

"I just want to look at you for a moment. I had no idea you were an accomplished pianist. What other talents have you kept to yourself?"

"None that I can think of. I taught piano for many years and perhaps when all is said and done and we are finished with the building and fields, I will start teaching some of the local children. Anything else you would like to know?"

"No, I'll wait for the next surprise. I want you to know that everything is going good and on time. You will have bumper crops of corn and broccoli. I've planted them in one section of land and peanuts in another. The largest section will be your sweet potatoes. I will have those in the ground soon and on their way. The alfalfa is up and growing quickly and before you can blink an eye we will need to mow and bail. We will only mow as much as can be bailed in one day. It is selling for a good price and you will make money with it. Luke has supplied me with men and he has kept their time checked for me. I am paying them every two weeks. I think you are going to be surprised and happy with the outcome of your farming venture. I believe it will prove to be worthwhile. Once we have seen how everything goes, we can choose the most profitable crop and plant more the following year. The people I am hiring will work one field and then another. You will need to employ more, and just look at all the tables you will be filling."

"That is the whole idea Kenneth, filling the bellies of many. Have you looked at the shed that will serve as a warehouse? They removed one of the walls to make it all one big room. Have a look at it and see if it is satisfactory."

"It is, I watched them work on it and I gave them directions and told them what material to buy. It is perfect." He studied her face, looked into her eyes and envisioned how she would feel in his arms. She was the kind of woman he wanted. A feeling of emptiness and aching need squeezed at his heart and he looked away.

Noticing, his expression she asked, "Is something wrong?"

He cleared his throat, "To be honest my mind drifted for a moment, thinking about the storage room and the potatoes. They will be sized for marketing. The ones that are not the right size are called culls, you can sell or give them to the people. They are just as good as the market size, sometimes better."

"Here, let me pour you another glass of lemonade. How about something else? Would you like a sandwich?"

"No thanks, I'll be getting along. I need to talk with Luke and check on the work in the field. I will see you another day." He looked at her adoringly, "There is nothing I wouldn't do for you Carol. Please know I will not let you down. I will see you through your farming project."

She put her hand on his and looked into his eyes. "I know you will Kenneth. I am so fortunate to have a fiend like you."

Her touch left him speechless. He turned and silently walked away.

Carol watching him leave noticed he was no longer awkward and was actually rather handsome, with piercing dark eyes that could not hide his feelings. What should she do? She hoped he would find someone and not live his entire life with no one but his mother.

He passed Sam's Uptown Cleaners truck on its way through the gate, smiled and thought to himself, 'She has unending energy.'

The Cleaner's truck circled the drive, stopped in front of Carol and Sam got out and greeted her. "My curiosity got the best of me, I thought I would personally deliver these and help my boy get them into your house."

"Wonderful, I'm anxious to get all the drapes up and everything in place. The third floor was delivered the other day. Just bring them in and I will call one of my men to help the ladies with them."

"Misses Savage, I was hoping you might allow me to have a look around."

"I surely will! First let me call Jacob." She went to the end of the porch and rang the bell once. A few minutes later Jacob appeared.

"You rang for me Miss Carol?"

"Yes Jacob, I want you to help the young man by the truck bring in the drapes and things for the rooms on the second floor. Put them all in the first suite and then go back to whatever you were doing."

"Yes Mam!" He turned and went to the truck and began to help the other young man get things out and in.

Sam asked how Jacob knew the bell was for him. "Oh," Carol replied, "I have one ring for Jacob, two for Mark and three for Luke. If I want all three, I ring it four times. In the event of trouble, I ring it and keep ringing and everyone comes. It was used to call the slaves in from the fields in the eighteen hundreds when the house was built. Now follow me and we will go up to the third floor. After that I will show you around some of the other finished rooms."

He fell in behind her, "I wouldn't want to climb these stairs everyday. I'm getting too old for this."

She laughed and opened the door to one of the suites. "All the suits on this floor are the same." She pulled aside the drapes and fastened them back. Sunlight flooded the room and it came alive with color. "These were guests suits with adjoining baths. I rather think families were given them side by side."

"My Lord, this is sumptuous! Made for royalty! I had no idea this old house held within its walls such classic aesthetic beauty! I would love to have my wife to see it."

"When all is complete, I will have an open house day for those who wish to see what they would have missed had it been destroyed."

"What do you plan to do with it? Are you going to turn it into a Bed and Breakfast?"

"I really have not decided. Your question has been asked by many. We, Paul, his mother and I will be moving in as soon as possible. After that I may decide what we should do with it. Who's to say? We are young and we may end up with a very big family." She laughed and caught him eying her body. "We have not yet begun." He blushed, embarrassed and she saved him. "Now come, I will show you some of the down stair rooms."

They first visited the small living room, the formal dining room and on into the main drawing room where he stopped and stared up at the life sized portrait of her grandmother. The French doors were opened and light streamed into the room. "Breathtaking," he said, "that is your grandmother, she was a beautiful refined lady. Everything in this house takes my breath away. The piano, the French doors opening out into the garden, the drapes and furniture, all are reminders of a cultural elegance and refinement of generations past. This house was built with much thought and love. Do you play the piano, or did your grandmother?"

"The piano is mine. I had it brought from my other home. I am a teacher. Perhaps I will teach again one day. Now, may I offer you a little refreshment while you are here?"

"Thank you, I think not," he handed her the bill, "you can pay this the next time you are in town. I need to get back to the store."

"I would rather give you a check for this now. Please, follow me into the study." She opened the door and went to the desk.

He stopped and glanced around at the shelves covered with books. "I can just picture old James in this room, sitting in that chair reading."

"Yes, so can I. It is a comforting room. When I'm tired I slip in, sit in his chair and doze off for a few minutes. For some unknown reason this room gives me courage." She handed him the check. "I do thank you for the care you gave to everything. You have brought them all back to me looking as if they made yesterday."

"I was happy to do it. They made things better in your grandparent's day. Thank you and I will be looking forward to your open house."

Gertie came up and stood beside her as he drove away. "He a nice man," she said, "now I thinks we needs to see'd them cabins out back."

They opened a door and went in. The cast iron pot hanging in the fireplace had been cleaned and polished, everything was clean and it felt empty. "Oh Gertie, this is dismal. We must do something to cheer these cabins up."

"Yes'm. Them beds needs patch work quilts and pillers to sits on in them rockers."

"You are right and some little curtains for the windows. Tomorrow I will shop. Today they make comforters that look just like old fashioned quilts. We also need to put some plates and things on the shelves and have Jacob bring in some fire wood and put it in the wood boxes."

"What fo? Ain't nobody live here?"

"Because Gertie, if the time ever comes when these little cabins are needed they will be ready and the beds will have soft mattresses."

"I guess? Is you specun some ghosts to move in?"

They both laughed, "Maybe they are already here Gertie."

"There you goes again! What kind'a ghosts is gonna hang round here?"

"A tired old slave, Gertie."

"Let me out!" Gertie grabbed her hand and pulled her out the door. "You is bond to stir up them ghosts ain't ya?"

After work she returned to town and Melba and Paul's cottage. As they sat at the table each talked about their day.

"My closet is almost empty," Melba said, "I am prepared to move in whenever you give us the go-ahead. I will put an ad in the paper and a sign out front: Furnished, Beautiful home, for rent or lease. I'll be here most of the time just in case someone drops in to look around. I will also put Paul's phone number in the ad and on the sign. If I am not here, he can show the house."

"Mom! I'm a working boy what makes you think I can take time off to show our house?"

She just smiled at him. "Because I know you will."

"Tomorrow, Melba, I would like you to go shopping with me. I need to buy a few things for the little cabins behind the house."

"Carol, whatever for? Do you expect to have someone living in them?"

"One never knows? They are nice little cabins and they may come in handy. She looked at Paul, "how was your day, honey? Did you think about me?"

"You bet! How could I get you off of my mind? I have a young couple who think they want a divorce. I think they are very much in love. The problem is the lady is a bit spoiled and wants a little more than the man can afford." He stopped and thought for a minute. "Now that gives me an idea. They are to return tomorrow afternoon. I will delve a little deeper into their problem and will mention this house, very nonchalantly of course, and I will mention that I have lived in it for many years and since I am newly married we are moving into another house. I will watch the lady's face as I talk about it and if she shows any kind of a spark, I will offer to show it and tell them it is for rent or lease at a very reasonable price with an option to buy."

"Paul," Melba objected, "what do you mean by reasonable and an option to buy?"

"The kind of price you and dad paid for our nice little home. Why would you not want to sell? You will be living in a mansion, with servants, friends and a cook!"

Melba laughed, "Well we have to have some money!"

"Let Paul take care of it Melba. We will be shopping and he could show them the house while we are out."

"You young folks are a bit quick for me. Still, it might be a good idea. I will leave the pricing up to you Paul and I trust you will not be too giving. If you are, they will think something is wrong with it."

They went to bed and Carol snuggled her nude little body against Paul's, and asked, "Am I getting fat?"

"Noooo, you are just right for me. Why do you ask?"

"Well Gertie asked if I had a bun in the oven and Kenneth viewed me like he thought I might be pregnant. Do I look pregnant?"

"No you don't. Are you?

"No silly. I would not keep a thing like that from you. We have never talked about having children. Do you like babies? Would you like to have children?"

"Yes, I would! And since we have that huge house to live in, I would like a dozen."

"What? Why so many?"

"Because I was an only child and I always wished I had a brother or sister."

"Maybe we should start working on it right now." She put a leg over his hip and he moaned.

"You really know how to start a family."

"Shut up and love me!"

The time had come. The potato plants were being placed carefully in rows and the fields were filled with men working and singing. It was as if time had been turned back to another age. Living in granddaddy's mansion was paradise. Paul had talked the young couple into staying together and they had leased Melba's house with an option to buy. Life was beautiful and life was growing inside Carol's belly.

"I think it's time for us to have that open house for the townsfolk," Carol announced, "I will start it around ten and by noon the street will be lined with people. After we have shown our historical estate, I will have a dinner for a selective few. Some of Melba's friends and of course the McFarlands and Chad, if he happens to be back from New York. I think he and Rose are an item. They are spending a great deal of time together. I've been told that Rose has been making quite a few trips to New York.

Later, when the crops are harvested and the new planting has begun, we will have lawn party for all the workers, blacks and whites. And that will be the best party of all because there will be singing and dancing and merrymaking like we have never seen or heard. I might invite the McFarlands because Jessie said she would love to hear the singing. But before all this takes place, we must have Kenneth and his mother over for a quiet dinner. He is such a dear person!I could not have done this without all his help."

Paul put his hand on her belly, "I know you love all this but don't you think it is about time for you slow down a little?"

"Nice feeling isn't it?" She put her hand on his, and said, "It is too soon for you to worry about me overdoing. I haven't even begun to show, have I?"

"Just to me, and I'll bet mom and Gertie."

"Oh yes, they noticed right away. My apple cheeks and a tiny little pooch in front told on me. My condition is another reason I feel we should have the open house and the dinners. I would like to do it while I am still able to walk erect."

"We are not going to stop with one baby are we?"

"No indeed not. You said you wanted a dozen so we will work on it."

"My pleasure," he replied, "lets see what our ghosts have to say about all this."

"They already know because they visit me while I am resting in the study. They are thrilled and I think granddaddy agrees with you. We should have a dozen."

The little cabins behind the house were shingled in blue, the fireplaces remained and central heating was connected from the house. Patch work comforters covered soft mattresses and patch work cushions were placed on the rocking chairs. Matching cafe pocket type curtains hung at the windows. The kerosene lamps remained in little brackets on the wall and similar electric lamps were placed on the tables. The cabins were complete without losing the feeling of the past. The floors had been cleaned and waxed and circular area rugs covered the center of the rooms.

Chad suddenly appeared on the scene and peaked in through the door. As usual he was looking like something off the cover of a mens magazine. He greeted Carol with a smile, a hug and, "My we are getting a little plump aren't we? Would you by any chance be?"

She stopped him, "Yes, I would be and it is not by chance. We are planning to have a large family to fill these happy halls."

"Is that what these charming little cabins are for?" He laughed.

"No. They were slave quarters a hundred years ago and I did not want them destroyed. If we ever need a little extra room, we will always have these."

"Charming idea, but with a home as big as this how could you possibly need extra room, unless you decide to use it for servants quarters. Is the house complete? If so, I would love to walk through it."

"You are welcomed any time Chad. I am having a dinner and inviting the McFarlands, and I do hope you will join us. I hear that you and Rose are becoming an item."

"Odd you should say that. I do have deep feelings for Rose. She is a fascinating lady but is accustomed to having her own way about everything."

"That should not bother you. She sounds like the perfect woman for you!"

"That is exactly the problem we are both spoiled and independent and want things our way. I, being a man, am rather resentful of women like yourself and Rose, who need not be dependent upon anyone. I am not like Paul. I cannot allow a woman to have the upper hand."

"Watch it Chad, you are treading on dangerous ground! Paul and I are a perfect blend, we know how to give and we know how to take. If Paul does not agree with me, he tells me and I do the same. Neither of us will be led by the other. He knew me before and is thrilled to see that I have not allowed life to beat me down. I suppose Rose, on the other hand, has never given thought to being without or having to do for herself. Yes, she is the perfect person for you because you can give her everything her little heart desires."

"And here we are sparring again. I thought all that would end when I gave up the idea of buying your land. I heard that McFarland gave you an extremely lucrative offer and you refused."

"I did. And I will continue to do so until he comes up with an offer I can't refuse."

"And what would that be?"

"I'll think about it! I am having a small dinner this coming Friday. The McFarlands have been sent an invitation and have accepted. Since you are here I am personally inviting you. Dinner will be at eight, would you like to join us?

"I would be delighted. I am anxious to be seated in your glorious dining room. Will Melba be preparing the meal?"

"Melba would love to do it all, however, I have employed a cook from New Orleans to prepare the dinner. Fortunately Bess, Fiona, Jacob and Mark worked for and served meals at the McFarland's. They are well versed in the protocol of serving. Gertie will be in the kitchen hanging over the shoulder of my New Orleans chef to make sure he knows what he is doing." She chuckled, "Gertie would like to cook the entire meal as would Melba, but I think this time I will leave it up to the professional. It is time for both Gertie and Melba to rest. We have all been working night and day."

"Ah, but you found time for love."

"Yes, I will always have time for love. Would you like to see the wine cellar? I have been stocking up on fine wines. My father was a wine connoisseur, I am not, but we have a few."

Chad walked along and began to read the labels, checking the year and exclaiming, "My dear these are all fine wines and very expensive. Just look at this: Champagne: Dom Perignon,

Armand De Brignac; Perrier Jouet; Veuve Cloquot. Red wines: Chambertin Grand Cru; Chateau Latour 2009 Lagrange; Chateau Gruaud-Larose; Chateau Margaux and Pichon - Longueville Pauillac Comtesse de Lalande; Petrus' Chateau Haut-Batailley and Chateau Montrose Latour Pauillac France 1990: Heavens! White wines: Domaine Ramonet Montrachet Grand; Domaine de la Romainee Grand Cru Conte Montrachet."

"I hope I have done well," Carol said. Most are French, but please do not overlook the Spanish and Portuguese wines. I'm not familiar with most of these wines. I simply did a little bit of research and pray I have bought palatable wines. We will allow our French chef to choose the wines for dinner."

Chad obviously impressed, continued to exclaim, "My dear, you have a fortune in some extremely fine wines!"

"Yes we do, but if kept at the right temperature I am told they will last another hundred years. I might add, I doubt we can live long enough to use it all."

"I am truly looking forward to this French Cuisine. Although, I doubt it will surpass Melba's expertise."

"She will be pleased to hear that. She loves experimenting with different recipes."

"I must tell you dear cousin, I am quite impressed with your courage and knowledge. You have turned this mansion into a castle. You were right. It should never be destroyed. I commend you on your foresight. Now I must leave as I have an engagement with Rose."

The harvesting had begun and soon everything but the sweet potatoes would be taken to market. Standing at the far corner of the porch, her gaze followed along the leafy hedges starred with dog-roses, she breathed in the sweet scent of violet, wisteria and jasmine. Thrushes fluttered about singing loudly and blackbirds squawked and flew away. Her dream was coming true. The fields were filled with laborers singing as they worked, their voices rising rhythmically as if following a drum beat. Things were moving swiftly and smoothly. A very tiny movement in her belly said it was time for a little tea and perhaps a crumpet or two.

Gertie was stirring a large pot of Filet Gumbo, she looked up at Carol and said, "Ain't nobody kin make gumbo likes me. I bet that French cook you done hired know nothin bout it!"

Melba asked, "Would you like a little tea and a bite to eat? You look a little peeked"

"Yes, and a couple of Gertie's biscuits with the bacon bits in them."

Melba poured them each a cup of tea and sat with her while Gertie brought the biscuits. "She won't let me look into the pot, or taste her gumbo, says it's a secret." She sipped at her tea. "Now when is that Frenchman supposed to arrive and where are you putting him?"

"In the servant's quarters right through

that door. You should know, you helped arrange those rooms. They are clean and ready to be occupied. What else could he need? He has his own bathroom, sitting room and a pleasant little fireplace. He is a cook! He cannot be stuffy or into himself, despite his fame."

"How long he gonna be here," Gertie asked.

"He would accept no less than two weeks."

Gertie grumbled, "You ain't needin him no how! You's got me an Miss Melba!"

Melba laughed, "I think Gertie is right! We could do this dinner for the McFarlands but I know why you are going to so much trouble. You want to make sure everything comes up to the dinner they served."

"Yes ladies you are right. I am going a little overboard with this. Still I know Gertie will have a ball in the kitchen fussing and fuming over everything. And you, Melba, will just sit and enjoy and help me entertain our uppity neighbors. It will be a very interesting evening. You bet, I want to impress them in the same style as my grandmother. Also, I'm anxious to hear what McFarland has to say about this house, the crops and the workers in the fields. Chad will be here joining them. I think he may be falling in love with Rose. Kenneth Dobbs and his mother have been invited and you will be talking with her."

"Oh I'm looking forward to this. Eunice is a very lovely lady and so is Jessie."

"Huh," Gertie grunted, "Sound like you is plannin a big night an I'is gonna be watchin your fancy cook. I guesses he gonna tell me bout cookin," she grumbled. "Huh!"

"Gertie," Carol replied, "for once in your life allow someone else to do the work! One day, after this dinner, we are going to have a big lawn party for all the field workers and it is going to take you, him, the girls, Melba and me to do the cooking and serving. Just think of how many there will be! I would like the Reverend and his family to come and all of your family and those who were at the party you had after church. It is going to take tons of food." She gave Gertie a pat on the rump, "I know you could do this dinner for the McFarlands, but how often have you told me your bones get tired? I think what you should do is sit down on a bench and enjoy the party."

"If you says so, but I'is keepin an eye on that cook! Do he know English?"

"Yes Gertie, he does, and he probably cooks your kind of food! I just thought since I would be entertaining the high and mighty I should give this a try. Why do you object Gertie? Don't you think it will be nice to take a little rest?"

"Ain't my place ta say nothin Miss Carol. But you's good an better as them folk. Ain't nobody nice is you."

"Thank you Gertie. Everyone gives me far too much credit. I am only doing what the Lord says I should."

"When you say he gonna be here?"

"I expect him to be here by Thursday. Now don't go jumping all over him. Try to get along. Maybe he can show you a thing or two, and maybe you can show him. So try to be nice."

"Hmm-mm, yes I'is."

"Come on Melba, let's go into the dining room and look things over. We'll use Grandma's white English Wedgwood and the gold rimmed charger plates. I want the table set complete with goblets and three wine glasses next to each plate. We will be serving more than one wine. The cook can choose the wines. Bess, Fiona and Jacob will serve, and Jacob will serve the wine wearing white gloves. The McFarlands employed them at one time, I wonder why they didn't keep them?"

"Carol, did you not notice they had no black help? I wonder why? Maybe Rose is prejudiced. Her father will do anything for her. If she didn't like them, they would have to go."

"We know Jessie would not have let them go because she said she loved their singing."

"Carol, are we impressing the McFarlands or Chad?"

"Both! He will never look down his nose at us again. I know I shouldn't feel that way but he made some disparaging remarks about my grandfather and my father and he needs to be spanked. It's a little late in years for it, but he does need a lesson."

"I agree!" Melba replied remembering his remark about her meatloaf.

"We will enjoy this but we will enjoy,

more, the lawn party with all the hired hands. Jessie will love it, too. She's not a stuffed shirt!"

"I think it's about time to get Bess in here and explain how I want the table set. I want a bowl of roses in the center, under the chandelier. I noticed some lavender ones in the garden, I would like those mixed with baby breath and white and pink carnations. We have a very large, long, oval shaped crystal bowl that when filled will be breathtaking. I don't want anyone straining to see over a tall bouquet. Our light indigo-blue table cloth will be placed beneath grandmother's white lace overlay and matching indigo-blue napkins will be placed alongside each setting. On the piano in the drawing room, I would like another bouquet of roses."

A voice came from the doorway, "Hey ladies you got a kiss for a tired man?"

"Is it that late? Time gets away from us. Kiss me and we'll get Gertie out of the kitchen. She made gumbo today."

A peck on the cheek for Melba and he took Carol in his arms, "How's my little mother doing? You haven't been lifting anything heavy have you?"

"Silly, no of course not! Now let's go get some gumbo. Follow me into the breakfast room, it's pleasant and filled with sunshine. I noticed Luke's truck is outside so Gertie can go home and take a big pot of gumbo with her for the children. Will you tell Gertie that, Melba, while I give this man a real kiss?"

"You bet! You two get comfortable and

I'll bring us each a big bowl of gumbo, a loaf of French bread and a bottle of red wine."

Paul put his hand on Carol's belly. "You know honey when you are farther along, I do not want you climbing the stairs. We will bunk down here in one of the servant quarters."

"Sounds fine to me, or we have those lovely little cabins out back with beds just about the right size for us to snuggle. We might even meet some new ghosts!"She giggled.

It was a perfect evening for the dinner. Cars entered and stopped in front of the house and Luke greeted them, helped the ladies out and took the cars a little farther around the drive.

The chandelier in the foyer gleamed in the light and lit up the eighteenth century designs in the wall paper. Mark took their wraps, and Paul escorted everyone into the drawing room.

McFarland stopped and gazed up at the portrait of the late Misses Nelson. "My word, she was a beauty wasn't she?

Jessie sat on one of the lounge chairs and followed his gaze. "She truly was. I remember dining here with her many times. She was not only beautiful, she was charming, big hearted gracious, gentle and kind. Carol, my dear, I am so happy to see it all restored. This home was built long before ours. I believe your grandfather left it to the right person. However, I do not recall your grandmother playing the piano."

"She did not, I do," Carol replied, and went to the piano and began to play 'To a Tear

Drop,' a melancholy tune lifted from one of Chopin's Nocturnes. The French doors were opened and the sweet scent of roses and night blooming jasmine filled the room.

Chad had been taken aback by Jessie's remark about the mansion being bequeath to the right person, but he said nothing. Rose listened to the melancholy excerpt and complimented Carol, "You play beautifully."

Chad found his voice: "My cousin never fails to surprise me! She is a woman with many talents. How long have you been playing?"

She smiled, "Many years. I did concert work and then became a piano teacher." She left the piano and joined them with a glass of wine. "At the moment my life is full and I hardly have time to play for my husband. She turned as Paul escorted Kenneth and his mother in. Looking at Jessie, she said, "I'm guessing you all know each other!"

Jessie exclaimed, "Why yes, we do! We have not seen each other in a long time and this is such a pleasant surprise."

Eunice smiled, "I have invited you many times and received no reply."

Jessie, humbly apologize, "I must have missed your invitations. I live a rather cloistered life."

Roy turned and glared at her. "Sorry my dear, her invitations must have slipped by me as I glanced through the mail. You know I tend to look at nothing but business letters."

"That's alright dear, I'm sure Eunice

understands. In the future I will ask the maid to bring the mail directly to me."

Carol sensed a very uneasy moment and tried to lighten the tension. "Tonight we are all in for a treat. I have hired a French chef from New Orleans, Emile Moreau, and I have allowed him complete freedom in the kitchen. Tonight's dinner will be a surprise for us all. I know it is my place to make the decisions but since he is quite famous I thought I would allow him the pleasure."

At that moment, Jacob appeared and announced, "Dinner is served."

Once seated at the dining room table, Jessie continued to exclaim with pleasure as she examined the diner wear, "Oh my, this is like old times. I remember this all so well. You have brought the past right through these doors. I can see your grandmother seated at one end of the table wearing a lavender gown, a long string of pearls and a large diamond broach at her throat, her hair pomp-ed and a chignon in the back, just as it is in the painting. She was so warm and charming."

Jacob entered with a light white wine, Picquepoul de Pinet, and with white gloved hands, filled their glasses very carefully, ladies first.

Paul stood up, raised his glass and looked at his wife seated at the opposite end of the table and said, "To my beautiful wife a thank you for this night. And to our guests, a welcome thank you for joining us. May this be the beginning of many more such occasions."

Raising their glasses, McFarland said, "Hear, hear! And what a joyous occasion it is!"

Bess and Fiona entered and began to serve. First they placed a small dish of crab meat in a creamy sauce in front of each and left the room, returned and stood quietly behind the guests and waited. A short while later they removed the plates and placed a small bowl of Shrimp Remoulade in its place.

Melba exclaimed, "This is delicious, I must ask how it is prepared!"

Again, the girls returned and removed the Remoulade plates and replaced them with small bowls of creole gumbo.

"Heavens," Jessie exclaimed, "if we eat all of this we won't have room for the entree!" Nevertheless, she ate, as did everyone.

The food continued to come: A small salad of iceberg-lettuce with Roquefort-dressing, steamed-buttered asparagus, puffed potatoes-fried and breast of chicken on thin slices of ham covered in Bearnaise sauce. Their glasses were filled with different wines to blend with each serving: Sancerre Bordeau, followed by Monopole Romanee Conti. As the Conti was poured, Carol caught Chad's expression as he glimpsed the Romanee-Conti label and gasped knowing the price. To hide his embarrassment he quickly covered his mouth with his napkin and Carol smiled.

After the entree's were finished and the dinner plates removed, the cart for the Cherries

Jubilee Flambe was brought in and Emile entered in full chef's attire, began to mix, flame and fill individual bowls as the girls took them and served. Accompanying the desert, Cafe' Brulot Diabolique was flamed and served.

McFarland spoke up, "I must compliment you my dear, I have never had such a fabulous dinner, nor have I tasted better wine!"

Jessie confirmed it with, "And it has all been served with such savoir faire!"

Unashamedly Melba said, "And I am going to learn how to do all of this."

Eunice mumbled, "Why bother to learn when you have Emile?"

Everyone laughed and agreed.

"Shall we return to the drawing room for an after dinner drink and added conversation?" Carol asked. "The night is young."

They partnered, entered and sat around the fireplace while Jacob served each a tiny glass Midori liqueur. Jessie sipped hers and said, "If possible, I would prefer a demitasse of New Orleans pure coffee. Not Cafe Brulot."

Jacob asked if any of the others would like the same and they agreed. He left and returned with a tray of delicate demitasse cups and two tall, French coffee pots. While they watched, he made the coffee, poured it, served each person and asked if they would like sugar and cream. "Never cream," Jessie replied, "but definitely sugar."

The food and drinks found everyone at ease and they settled into laughter and general conversation. McFarland followed Carol to the piano and sat beside her while Paul watched with amusement. "Ahem,"McFarland cleared his throat, "I've been watching everything you have been doing with the land. Have you given further thought to selling me the piece I want?"

"Have you forgotten? We've had this conversation before! One Million Five hundred thousand!"

"You can't be serious,"he blustered.

"I am very serious Mister McFarland, take it or leave it."

"I will leave it," he replied, and in a huff left the piano and went to Jessie, "My dear, I think it must be time for us to leave."

Puzzled she got up and went to Carol, "I am sorry to say we will be leaving now. The dinner was superb! I thank you so much for asking us to join you for such lovely evening."

Carol got up and walked with her through the room and Paul joined them. "I'm sorry to see you leaving so early," he said, as Chad and Rose followed.

"The master has spoken,"Jessie replied.

"We also, must be leaving, "Chad said. "It has been an awesome evening filled with surprises. We thank you."

McFarland glanced at Carol, and said, "Reconsider."

She smiled, "I hope you will join us again. And Jessie, perhaps you will be able to talk Roy into allowing you to join us when we have our end of the harvest party. There will be singing and dancing."

"I would love it! Please let us know when."

Kenneth and Eunice, joined the others to bid them goodnight. "We have never had such a wonderful evening, thank you."

After they left Paul asked, "What was all that at the piano?"

"A million five hundred thousand."

Paul laughed and put his arm around her, "Well my dear little wife, you certainly did it! Tonight, your cousin got his comeuppance."

"It was worth it, but I must confess, I am very tired and ready for bed." Nonetheless, they and Melba headed for the kitchen and found much laughter going on between Gertie and Emile. "Miss Carol, this man is some kind a cook! I'is learn from him."

"Madame is too kind. She has also taught me things and made me laugh?"

They said goodnight to all and Melba headed for her suite. Paul and Carol returned to the drawing room and sat on the floor in front of the fireplace.

A sudden burst wind closed the French doors. "My heavens! I wonder what caused that?" A ghostly figure stood beside the piano and Carol got up. "Who are you? What do you want?"

The figure moved toward her and stopped.

"I know you are here for a reason and you are trying to give me a message. What is it?"

The figure came near, touched her belly and moved away.

Carol gasped, "Oh God! What could she mean?" She glared at the figure and said, "Do not try to frighten me! Leave this house and never return. You are from hell! Get out!"

The French doors opened and closed and the figure was gone.

She fell into Paul's arms. "I have never had anything like that happen. Not even when I lost my mother and father. It frightens me."

He held her close, "Nothing can hurt you my love, not as long as you are in this house and in my arms. We have all our friends with us, look up at your grandmothers picture."

She looked up and it looked as if there were a tears in her grandmother's eyes. "What could it mean?"

"It means it is time for us to retire and for you not to worry. There is nothing but love in this room and this house and it will protect you from all else."

She looked again at the picture, and the tears were gone.

Carol's pregnancy had begun to show and she found herself wearing loose blouses and struggling into her jeans. "Got to find me something a little more comfortable," she said, "Melba let's go shopping!"

The next day while shopping they found themselves surrounded by ladies. All wanted to tell Carol how fabulous the house was and how thrilled they were that she had not destroyed it.

She was home with old school friends reminding her who they were and explaining their married life. Most had several children and some had a toddler hanging onto their skirts. It was a nice day and while lunching at a sidewalk cafe many of Melba's friends joined them. Her secret was out and their very own lawyer was going to be a father. This news did not go over well with Shirley, at the candy shop. 'It should have been me,' she thought.

Things were on the way to market. The potatoes were dug and boxed and stacked in the warehouse until time for delivery. The field had been gleaned and every worker's family had potatoes to last them a very long time.

With Gertie's help Emile got the food ready for the yard party. He loved it and joined in with the ladies as they sang. Mark and the men set up the tables on the lawn and turned it into a picnic ground. Carol sent a message to the McFarlands and asked if they would join the party. "Come in leisurely attire because this is a down home affair." To her surprise they accepted and so did Chad and Rose.

Kenneth and Eunice came early to help with everything and Eunice and Melba fluttered around making sure every one had a place to sit.

The Reverend and his wife and family were seated at one of the main tables, along with all the others from his church. When it looked as if all were seated, he stood up and in a very loud voice began, "Praise the Lord!" and all those from his church echoed his words. "I am asking the Lord to bless this food and everyone at these tables. This is a joyous evening because of this lady and her husband," he bowed toward Carol and Paul, "they have made all this possible. Thanks be to God!"

"Hallelujah," the people chanted.

"Homes have food,"he continued, "the bellies of our babies are filled and we all have reason to thank our Lord! Praise be to God!"

"Yes, Lord, hallelujah," they echoed.

"Now let us all get ourselves around the food and fill our plates!"

There was a rush to the food tables filled with everything mentionable. Laughter filled the air and everyone talked at the same time. McFarland eased up to Carol, and asked, "Have you changed your mind about that price?"

"No sir I have not!"

He grumbled and sat down beside his wife, "You are as stubborn as your grandfather."

"I thank you," she replied, "I enjoy being compared to him."

Jessie quietly snickered and shoved a piece of cornbread in her mouth, not daring to look at Roy.

As the dining slowed, the music began and voices rose up to the heavens, but not all was church music, most was New Orleans Cajun hoedowns. Mark played his Concertina and people got up from the tables and danced, even Jessie and Roy did a little jig. The party went on for hours and Emile grabbed Gertie and danced a few steps with her while clapping his hands to the sound of the Cajun hoedowns.

"I have never enjoyed working so much! This is a wonderful place," he said, "and the people are fantastic!"

It grew late and a cloud darkened the sky, the Reverend said another prayer and thanked Carol and Paul, "God gave us this beautiful night, "he shouted, "and now I think he wants us to return to our homes."

Obediently, his congregation collected food from the tables, thanked Carol and Paul and left, a few at a time.

Jessie, Roy, Rose and even Chad came to Carol and Paul and admitted they had never enjoyed themselves more. Kenneth and Eunice prepared to leave and Kenneth said, "I will see you tomorrow and we will talk over the sales."

Melba helped clear the tables and excused herself as she was tired and ready for bed. "I love you children, but I've had too much food and too much wine. I must sleep."

Paul and Carol left everything for Emile, Gertie and her family to clean up, and went into the study for a visit with grandaddy.

As they sat there holding one another and talking over the evening, little stars appeared and circled a picture behind grandfather's desk. At first they watched and smiled until Carol grew tense and looked at it closer. It was a picture of her great-great grandmother and grandfather standing beside Blue Manor. She suddenly felt cold, "Paul, something bad is about to happen!"

"Oh honey, I think you are imagining things. They don't look unhappy to me! You are over tired and we need to retire."

"I'm telling you Paul, they are trying to tell us something."

The stars danced up and down and kept circling the picture. "I think I know what they are telling us. Get that book of my grand-daddy's out of his desk and look at some the pictures in the album and see what is written under them."

He went to the desk, switched on a light and began to turn pages in the book. Finally he came to the same picture as the one on the wall. Under it was written, "The year of the great flood, everything on the low ground destroyed. First the wind, rain and then a cloud that roared in and swept everything in sight away. We lost many, but were able to save a few here in this house."

"I knew it!" she said, "we've got to warn everyone. Are Gertie and the boys still in the yard?"

"Yes, they are out there singing and working but their wives and children have gone home."

"Come quickly we must tell them."

They rushed out and Carol said, "Stop! Everyone stop! We are about to have a storm. Luke and Jacob, I want you to go to your village and warn everyone. Tell the Reverend to gather all the families together, collect all the canned food and water they can and get to a safe place. Probably the church because it is on a hill."

Luke spoke up,"Miss Carol, what makes you think there is a storm coming?"

"I just know Luke, and you must trust me. And Mark you go up to McFarland's and tell him to get all his horses out of the field and put them in their stalls in the barn. Now all of you get a move on."

"But Miss Carol, McFarland is not going to believe me," Mark replied.

Gertie said, "You gots to make him. If Miss Carol say it gonna happen – it gonna!"

Carol said. "McFarland is a superstitious Scotsman and if you tell him Miss Carol has insight he will believe you. Now get a move on and just leave things right where they are. After you talk to the Reverend and McFarland I want you three to bring your families back here to this house. Here is where you are going to stay until all this is over. Paul, call Kenneth and tell him a storm is coming and to take cover and get everyone he can together and into a safe place."

"He is going to think I'm crazy, Carol!"

"Paul, you know I am right, now don't you want Kenneth and Eunice to be safe?"

"Yes, I will somehow convince him."

The night continued to darken and Mark, Luke and Jacob were off warning people. The Reverend did not question. He said if Miss Carol says a storm is coming, it is, and he immediately sent someone to bring his people to the church.

Luke got his wife, Jacob got his wife and children and, also, Mark's wife and all his children and they returned to the mansion. Meanwhile Mark, at McFarland's had trouble convincing Roy there was a storm coming. He objected and said Carol was imagining things, nevertheless, after Mark left he called the stable boy and told him to round up all the horses and stock and bring them in.

When Gertie's family returned Carol said, "Get all the shutters closed and nail them down. Quickly as possible nails and hammers were brought from the tool shed, the shutters were closed and nailed to the wall and Carol called everyone, including Emile, into the drawing room. "I know you think I have lost my mind because I am with child but if my husband believes me then you all must trust in me. I have had a warning and I know something terrible is about to happen. You and your children are safe here in this house. Now that everything is locked down you can find rooms and go to them and sleep. If you do not wish to do that, we can all remain in this room until morning."

Everyone chose to remain with her and all found couches and chairs to recline on while the children lay on the floor in front of the fireplace and slept. For them, it was another picnic.

As morning came and daylight began to break, Luke peaked out through a tiny slit in one of the shutters. "Miss Carol, everything is orange out there. You are right, we are about to get it."

Suddenly there came a roar like a half

dozen trains on one track and all sounded as if they were headed straight for them. Everyone lie down flat on the floor, "Carol screamed, "Now!" There followed a horrible sound of moaning andcrashing and they could hear the shingles ripping off the outside walls. Babies began to cry and their mothers pulled them up against them and put their arms over them to protect them. "It's alright Carol shouted! We are safe, it is just the wind taking away the shingles, the house will stand and you are all safe!"

As quickly as it came, it subsided and torrents of rain pounded on the roof.

Luke said,"It has past and now there is nothing but rain."

Carol looked at Gertie, she had turned pale. "Gertie are you alright?"

Gertie caught her breath, "Yes Miss Carol. I'is gonna live, fo now." She began to breathe a little easier and Carol breathed a sigh of relief. "I want you all to stay put while Paul, I and the men have a look outside."

They went to the front door and eased it open. Rain was bucketing off of the roof onto the driveway and running down the hill to the gate where it turned the street into a fast moving river.

"The river,"Luke yelled,"is going to overflow and flood everything! It will fill up fast with this rain and wind and sweep everything away!"

Carol took Paul's hand, "Yes, we know Luke. But we are safe and we will remain safe.

We must pray for all the people in your village. Pray that the Reverend has them in the church. Do you think the church is strong enough to stand under all this wind and rain?"

Luke cried out,"Lord, I pray they didn't get that twister. I pray it didn't touch down on them the way it did on us. If it didn't, the church is high enough that the water won't reach them. If they brought all their canned foods and water, they will be all right. God will protect them."

Days followed and no communication with the outside world. Finally, one day they looked down the hill and saw a boat tied to the gate and Kenneth making his way up the hill. They met him at the door. He shook himself off and in a rush of words, said, "It's a miracle! Carol, you have saved the lives of many people. Almost everyone in the city is safe, except those who refused to believe me when I said a storm was coming. Buildings are flattened. It touched down, picked up and touched down again in different areas. A family of five died because they refused to believe. Nearly everyone else is safe even though some have injuries. I don't know how you knew but I thank God you did! I was told to give you a message. I passed by McFarland's on my way here to see if they were all okay and he said I should thank you, his horses are all safe. Now I need to get back into town. I am going around from house to house to see if there are still people to rescue. I went into your village Gertie, and everyone is in the church singing and praising the Lord. They have a couple of beat up boats alongside the church, so if they need help they can get it. There is no power. The city is working and trying to get things going again. It will take a few of days."

"We are fine," Paul assured him. "We have a generator, candles, lamps, fireplaces and wood burning stoves. We are in good shape. Do you want me to go with you?"

Carol looked alarmed but said nothing, and Kenneth noticed, "No I think you had better stay here with your wife and your very large family. As soon as the power is on, I will give you a call."

Carol breathed a sigh of relief. "Thank you Kenneth for everything."

"I hope your potatoes are high and dry," he said.

"I'm sure they are. We got everything else sold just in time. Thanks to a picture on the wall."

He looked confused but did not ask, just smiled and said, "We surely did."

"What picture?" Gertie asked. "You been talkin at them ghosts again?"

"No Gertie, it's just a picture that gave me a premonition."

"Hmm – mm!" Gertie said, "I knowed it! Them ghosts is here!. I knowed I see'd em! Nearly scared me to death."

Paul looked at Carol and smiled. "I guess they did Gertie!"

"Now listen everybody, we are all going

to be here for some time. You men can start opening the shutters and you ladies staying with your children in the rooms upstairs, make sure the children are behaving themselves. I want you all to be comfortable, but keep those rooms neat. You can light the fireplaces, but make sure the children stay away from them."

Gertie said, "I be stayin on the chairs jus like I be. I ain't sleepin in no room up them stairs. Sticks me in one a them cabins out back, me and the girls."

"Okay Gertie, you can have your way. But first we have to see if those buildings still have a roof on them."

Mark, Luke and Jacob said, "we'll find out when we are undoing all the shutters. Some of the upstairs ones were closed but not nailed, it was too dark and too dangerous for Jacob to get out there and nail them down. But they were closed and everything is alright. We will check everything right now." They headed for the upstairs rooms and found some of the shutters ripped back, but the windows were not broken and everything was dry. Jacob went into into the attic and came back,"There's some leaks in the attic that we'll have to fix but they ain't hurting nothing."

From there they checked the little houses in the back, looked in and found everything dry. Some shingles had pulled away from the walls and a few were gone from the roofs, still everything was dry. Jacob laughed, "Grandma should be right at home in one of these places. Matter of fact, I wouldn't mind staying in one with my wife."

Luke answered, "I'm sure if you tell Miss Carol, she will say it's okay. And it would be good for you to be near your grandma."

Children were running up and down the stairs and jumping on the beds in their rooms with their mothers scolding, "Get yourselves down off those beds and act like you've had some fetchin up! Do not bounce on the beds and do not put your shoes on the furniture." They giggled and all did as told. "And stay away from the windows, we don't want to pick any of you up off of the ground!"

Despite the storm, the house was filled with laughter and happiness. Emile was happy and able to cook because the stoves were gas, and a couple were old wood stoves like the ones his mother used. He made bread and pastries and shouted at the kids to not jump and cause his cakes to fall. Once when Carol followed the scent of fresh baked bread into the kitchen he said, "Madam, I would love to live here with you. This has been a marvelous experience. I have never witnessed more love and happiness."

"If you really mean that why don't you stay and let me put you on a regular salary."

He was hesitant, "I have a reputation and you know I am expensive. I have a family and my children are in school in New Orleans. I will have to give it some thought."

"Well perhaps you can consider our life style and your comfort and decide which is more important. Just let me know what you decide. Since you have a family, you could bring them and we can open the other quarters. We can take out a wall and make it into a complete apartment." She grabbed a small loaf of French bread, dipped it in some garlic-butter and olive oil and left the room. Outside the door she called back, "This is delicious!"

A couple of children ran up to her, "Has he got any cookies, Miss Carol?"

"I don't know, why don't you ask?" As she walked away she could hear him talking to them in French. If you want these cookies you must ask me in french. 'plaire un biscuit'.

"No we want a cookie!"

"Then you must say what I said."

She laughed and walked away eating her bread. "He is going to teach them all French?" Outside, she walked around the porch and down the stairs, backed off and looked up at the building. "Lord, we have a lot of mending to do," she grumbled, "and the entire thing will have to be painted again. That wind even ripped the paint off of things. No matter, thank you God, we are safe and healthy."

Something moved in her belly, she reached for the railing on the porch and slowly pulled herself up the steps and found a turned over porch chair, straightened it, sat down and belched, "Guess I shouldn't have had that bread," she said, "I think I'm going to be sick." Looking toward the other end of the porch she saw the same figure she had seen by the piano.

"Go away!" she screamed.

Gertie came looking. "Miss Carol, did I hears you call? You ain't lookin good! You sick?"

"Yes Gertie I am. I guess this is what they call morning sickness!"

"Oh! You is gonna has a girl!"

Carol laughed, "Now you made me feel better. Just walk with me. I want to go into the little living room and sit by the fire."

Worried, Gertie said, "Yes mam,"and walked alongside her. "Now you sits on this couch an I git Jacob. Ain't no fire in here an it damp."

Carol nodded.

"I wants you ta lay down on the sofa."

Carol stretched out on the couch and Gertie placed an afghan over her. "I be right back." She left the room and called for Jacob to find Paul. "Miss Carol need him, she sick. She layin on the sofa."

Paul dropped what he was doing and rushed to her side. "Carol, honey what is it?"

She could hardly speak, "I think I am going to lose the baby. You need to take me to our room and call Melba."

He picked her up, held his arms and carried her up the stairs and into their room and laid her on the bed. "Let me get these clothes off of you and tuck you in."

"Oh Paul," she moaned, "help me. Please, help me."

He tried to comfort her but he was afraid and didn't know what to do. He called for Melba

"Come quick!"

Gertie returned to the living room, found she was gone and called for Bess. "Find Miss Carol! She sick!"

Bess rushed up the stairs and found Carol writhing in pain. Carol reached for Melba's hand, "I am losing my baby, help me!"

Bess pushed Paul out of the room,"Find Fiona and tell her to bring us some hot water and towels. We need them, and see if the phone is working. If it is call the doctor."

Carol screamed as the door closed behind Paul. "It's too soon! Too soon! Please God, it's too soon."

Melba pulled back the covers as the fetus pushed out of her body."You are going to be all right honey," Melba said, "it's over. You lost your little baby, but God will bring you another. You have done too much work, you have taken care of everyone and the storm upset you. Now you are going to rest. Now you just lie back and let us clean you up."

Too late Fiona entered and Bess said, "Just help us get her cleaned up, then go down and get some brandy and bring it up to her. Tell Mister Paul to come in. I think she needs him more than anything else."

Fiona left the room crying and told Paul to enter. He found Carol weak and crying. Melba covered her and told him about the child. Tears filled his eyes. He leaned over Carol and kissed her and Melba left the room.

Carol reached up to him, "I'm so sorry

Paul. I lost our baby."

He held her in his arms. "It is not your fault. We will have another."

"Don't stop loving me Paul,"she pleaded.

"If we never have another child, I will still love you. Nothing can stop me from loving you."

She was sobbing when Fiona returned with the Brandy. "Bess says she needs to have this. It will help her sleep."

He held it to Carol's lips. "She is right honey, sip on this and soon you will rest." They were both crying and he held her until she slept.

Two days later she was up and out of bed and went into the study, pulled down an album and began to thumb through it. On one of the pages was the picture of a child in a coffin, she read under it. My dear little girl died at birth. My first child and only girl. Now Carol knew, the ghost was her grandmother trying to warn her. She closed the book and went in search of Paul. He was with the boys, giving directions. When he saw her, he asked,"Should you be out of bed?"

"Hold me Paul and tell me, what was our child, a girl or a boy?"

"A very tiny little girl."

She laid her head against his chest. "We'll be all right now honey. We will have two sons and we will name them James and Paul." It was not until after they had their first son that she told him about the ghost of her grandmother.

The water was subsiding and galloping

up the driveway came Roy McFarland.

"My word! How did you manage to get here through all that water?"

"I just road along the high spots. We had no trouble at all. My horse is sure-footed."

"Well come into the house with us and we'll fix you a spot of tea or coffee."

"I'll have coffee and you can top it with brandy and maybe that chef of yours has some sort of special delight to go with it."

"Sit yourself down and I'll see about it." She went into the kitchen and returned with a pot of coffee and a platter of Beignets covered in powdered sugar. "How's that?"

He laughed and reached for a doughnut, "Fabulous, now you and Paul sit with me and I will tell you why I have come."

She poured them each coffee and they all had a doughnut. "So…?"

"So you can get the contract out. You win. You are a touch lady. I am doubling that million five hundred thousand for the property. I am here to give you a check. Paul, you can draw up the papers. My checkbook is in my pocket and it's dry," he laughed.

She and Paul nearly choked, "Are you serious?"

"Yes, I am very serious! You saved me several million by telling me to bring in my horses. One of those horses has won several million dollars and if I had lost him, God only knows how much more I would have lost."

She laughed, "In that case maybe I should

have asked for more!"

"Carol, he has just given you more!" Paul exclaimed, and turned to Roy, "I will go into grandfather Nelson's office and draw those papers up right now." He winked at Carol. "They may be there already!"

While he was gone several children came and stood next to Mister McFarland and stared at the Beignets. One asked, "Sil vous plait puis-je avoir un beignet?"

"Are these Emile's children?"

"No, but each day he teaches them a little French. These are a few of the orphans that live with Mark."

He handed them each a doughnut and said, "Now run and tell Emile we need more."

They scurried off, leaving a trail of powdered sugar behind them."

"Orphans, are they? White children! Are you planning to adopt them?"

Paul returned, "Adopt who?"

"Roy wants to know if we are going to adopt some of the orphans?"

"Not a bad idea," he said, "and shoved some papers in front of Roy. We really want a large family and if we add a couple to our own, why not?" He kissed Carol, "What better mother could they have?"

She said nothing about the loss of their first born and McFarland did not seem to notice she was no longer carrying. Papers signed, he handed her a check for three million dollars.

"You are a tough lady but you have

brought good fortune to us. Were it not for you I might have lost all my stock and horses in that storm. I hope this check will help you with all your endeavors."

She took it and thanked him. "Now you can be happy, you finally have the land you have wanted so badly." She leaned over and gave him a kiss on the cheek. "Now that you have it, what do you plan to do with it?"

"I am adding an extra track for training my horses, six furlongs or two thousand three hundred twelve meters with a straight of four hundred fifty meters. I have been working them in a close area and this will be grand! Nearly all of my land is hilly and that's why I've wanted that stretch of property, it's flat. You probably don't know what I am talking about but Rose does and she is thrilled. Bless you my dear. You have made us very happy. You have also saved many lives. I question how you knew this storm was coming? In Scotland we would say you were in touch with the Spirits! Was old Nelson Ulster born?"

"No, but my great-grandmother was born in Ulster, Ireland."

"Ah, that explains it. You have inherited the witchcraft of the Irish"

Carol began to laugh, "Lord, don't let Gertie hear you say that! She is convinced this house is haunted!"

"I think she is right!" he laughed, "but I am happy to say you have inherited the soul of a good witch. I'll be off now. I've got a bit of water to go through. It should be gone in a few more days, as soon as the river goes down." He road off, high and proud on his Russian Budyonny.

"Well my little witch, I learn more about you everyday."

"Sure and does it surprise you?" she asked laughing with a bit of an Irish brogue.

"Not in the least. You have bewitched me for many years."

"Let's go into the kitchen and see what Gertie and Emile are up to. He has yet to tell me about his decision to stay or leave. Maybe we can get him to join with us like a family and sit at the kitchen table. Talk about bewitching, he has all the children hypnotized and learning French." They could hear the laughter as they entered.

Sitting at the table used by the help, Gertie and Mark's children were blowing sugar off the beignets, laughing and exchanging words in French with Gertie.

"Gertie," Carol said, "chase these little ones outside. The sun is shinning and they should be outside playing. We are lucky, there is no standing water in the yard!"

"Yes mam!"She turned to the children, "Allon, allon – nous allon," and in English she said, "come on chillen, we go! You's had eats, now git on out. When we gits dry, gonna be school agin! Look like we be goin home soon."

"Oh Gertie, don't be to sure of that! We don't know what is left of your homes. They might be all gone. The men need to find a way to get down there and see how things are. They have been spending all their time here putting things back together. We have not had a word from the Reverend, which means they could be big trouble even at the church. I wish Kenneth would have told us something about it. Paul, why don't you get Luke and the boys and see if you can make it down to the village."

"Anything you say love. It will take us awhile because I don't know how far we can go in the boat and we might have to walk and wade though water or swim if it gets too bad."

"I don't want you to swim! There are snakes in the water. Let us pray there will be enough high ground for you to get through without getting down deep in water."

"There is one little bridge to cross in order to get into the village! We must hope it hasn't washed away. If it has we will have to come back because that water is running fast and swift. It will take us quite awhile so don't get upset if we don't return until sundown." He laughed, "One of your ghost will let you know how we are."

Gertie screamed, "Is you see'd ghosts?"

"Gertie," Carol replied, "don't listen to him, he loves to tease!"

"Is you sho?"

"Paul, tell Gertie you were making a joke."

"Gertie, I was teasing you. I haven't seen a ghost since yesterday!"

Gertie rolled her eyes, "You see'd one

yesterday?"

"No Gertie, he did not! Now Paul, you stop that!"

He gave Gertie a hug, "No ghosts here Gertie, I was just joshing you."

"Huh," she grunted, "you better be cause I knows they's ghosts in this house cause I'is see'd em! Miss Carol say she chase-em out, but she ain't!"

"Okay honey, I'm going to get the men and leave. We will be as fast as possible. You just hold down the fort and do not worry. Please."

"I'll try." Melba held her hand as they watched them get into the little motor boat tied down by the gate and waved as they left. The day wore on and she began to worry as a soft rain began to fall.

"Here come the rain agin Miss Carol!" Gertie exclaimed, "I wish them mens a'git back."

"So do we Gertie. We don't need more rain." She sat on the porch and prayed for it to stop. "God, we do not need more rain. I am begging you to hear me. We do not need more rain. I know it's just a drizzle but we don't need it." She scanned the driveway and as she strained her eyes to see through the mist she saw something and heard the sound of an engine.

Gertie yelled, "They's back Miss Carol!"

And they were, all four, dragging up the driveway their boots and clothing covered in mud, their shoulders sagging with fatigue.

Carol threw her arms around Paul, "You said not to worry but I did. All of you go into the kitchen and get something hot to drink and something to eat. You look like you have just returned from the war."

"We have," Paul replied, "we really had to battle our way into the village and when we got there we found nothing. Their little shacks are all gone. Everyone is safe in the church, but they have nothing to return to."

"Yes Paul, they will. They will all come here. We will take care of them until we can rebuild their homes. We can build a tent city, and Emile, Melba and all the ladies can cook for everyone. Reverend can do his preaching in a tent. It may not be the first time. Once the rains have completely stopped, it won't take long to rebuild their little village. God is good! That's why McFarland gave me that check. You see? Everything has a reason!"

They went into the kitchen and crowded around the servants table. Luke was crying, "Lordy mama, I ain't never seen nothing like it! Everything is gone. If the church wasn't on that hill all our people would be dead."

Melba asked, "How many, Luke?"

"There are forty, maybe fifty families and their kids. We don't have tents for that many people!"

"How much lumber do we have in the sheds?" Carol asked.

"Not enough to build that many shacks!"

Paul said, "No we don't have enough for that, but we do have enough to build one large building. We could do that and put bunks in it for everyone. The ladies can cook outside on the barbeque pits and we can set up tables just like we did for the party. The reverend and his wife can have one of the suites in the house. Keep your faith, everything will work out fine. Come daylight, we will get in our boat and go back. We can start bringing people a little at a time. The reverend has a couple of boats tied up near the church. With three boats it won't take us long. We will start at day break."

"Hallelujah! You done save our people," Gertie cried.

"You all need to eat, take hot showers, rest and worry about all this in the morning. Paul is right; we have enough lumber to make a building big enough to take care of everyone. Luke, you and Paul can get started in the morning. Mark and Jacob can get those hammers and start building. In the meantime, until it is built, people can sleep on the floors, chairs and couches in the hallways. We will put as many as we can in the suites and the cabin out back. With the help of the man upstairs we will take care of everyone."

"What man upstairs? Gertie asked.

Carol laughed, "God, in heaven, Gertie!"

Emile started filling bowls with gumbo and Bess and Fiona sat a bowl in front of each man. Gertie got several loaves of French bread and put them on the table with a bowl of garlic butter and Melba brought in a bottle of brandy to top their coffee. "You'll need this to warm your bones and relax your bodies," she said.

Carol sat beside Paul, poured herself a glass of wine and said, "Before you start to eat and drink, we must say the blessing."They bowed their head and Carol blessed, "Bless us oh Lord for these thy gifts which we are about to receive from thy bounty, through Christ Our Lord. Bless and take care of all those who are marooned in the little church in the village. And thank you Lord for your messenger who has saved us from this storm." She squeezed Paul's hand.

Melba stood in front of them and smiled, "The luckiest day of our lives was the day you returned to us Carol. Love and joy follow you wherever you go."

Emile looked at Carol, "Yes, love and joy follow you, but 'mon dieu' look what you have done to me! When can I bring my family?"

"What? You mean you have decided to stay?"

"Madam, how can I leave a place with so much love. A home that needs me? I want very much to stay. And Melba needs me. She is going to learn to cook French style and she is going to learn to speak French. If the children can do it, so can she!"

Melba laughed and agreed, "You also need me Carol, to help with the children."

The next morning at dawn Paul looked down at the street from the balcony. "Come here honey and have a look. That little bit of rain we had caused no harm. The water has receded enough to allow us to take Luke's truck. We may be able to drive as far as the bridge. I wouldn't think of trying to drive across it. If we can get that far we can take groups of people from the church and bring them back a few at a time. With luck we'll be able to get them all here by nightfall. Meanwhile, have Emile, Melba and the girls cook up as many large pots of red beans and rice as possible because those folks have not had hot food since the storm began. And get out as many blankets and things as you can, and sweaters and dry clothes of some kind, any kind, because they have nothing but the things on their backs!"

"I love you so much," Carol said, "please be safe."

"I love you more," he replied, "and I'll be safe just for you."

They dressed, went down stairs and Paul said, "I'll get something to eat then get Luke and we'll be off."

Gertie came in grumbling and blinking her eyes, "We's up mighty early! Ain't near day yet!"

"Gertie, the men are eating and then Luke and Paul are going to drive to the village and start bringing people here."

Gertie peered through the morning haze, "They is? Don't look good to me!"

"It's okay Gertie, the water has receded and they can make it to the bridge. In the meantime Melba and the rest of us will cook up some pots of beans and rice for the families."

"Lordy! I gots to eat me somethin first!"

"Sit down and Emile will feed you."

Melba gave Gertie a hug, "As long as we have you Gertie, we are all happy. You have been in this house for how many years?

"I cain't member!"

"Well do you remember how old you are?"

"How ole is I Bess?"

"You will be one hundred years old next birthday."

Gertie began to laugh, "That make me feel ole!"

Paul and Luke left and Jacob and Mark headed for the tool sheds and worked feverishly through the day. The first truckload of women and children arrived and headed straight for the scent of cooked beans. Gertie handed each an empty bowl and they lined up and waited for it to be filled. With a piece of cornbread and their bowl of beans and rice, they found a spot on the porch where they could sit.

"Jus look at them chillen," Gertie said,"they half starved." And to the children she said, "Afore you eats them beans you all thank the Lord and praise him cause right where you is sittin you be sleepin. If you needs more beans you git up to that kitchen door and Bess will fill you bowl."

"They will not be sleeping outside Gertie. They will be sleeping inside, in the hallways and in the rooms, on the floors and in the chairs, but they will not be outside in the cold. It is warm during the day but at night it gets cold. Just look at these pitiful children. They are dirty and still in shock. We need to take turns and bathe them and get some dry clothing on them. We don't have anything that will fit, but they can wear all the things we have been taking out of grandma's closets. Grandma saved my daddy and uncle's small clothes, it will fit some. I knew it would come in handy! The clothes they are wearing can be washed and dried and tomorrow they can put them on. Food and a hot bath will warm their little bones. And when the bigger girls put on grandma's dresses and the bigger boys put on grandpa's pants they will think they are playing house."

It was nearly dark when the last load arrived with the Reverend and his family. He viewed the mothers and children and began to pray and sing and everyone joined in.

As each truckload of families arrived, the men grabbed a piece of cornbread, a bowl of beans and rice, ate, and went to work helping Mark and Jacob. The floor of the building was in and the frame work was up. With luck, the next day it would get walls and a roof.

"Joy!" The Reverend shouted loudly, "Joy and great love has come to us! Thank you Lord! Praise be to God!" The people began to sing, "Faith is Our Victory, Faith overcomes all!"

That night Paul pulled Carol close and made love to her. "Now we have started the rest of our family."

"You are such a love Paul. Yes, we will

have our family. You are strong and you are good. Melba says you are just like your father. I love her and her big heart. She helps everyone and she was there for me in my need."

"That's mom! She loves every minute of it. She loves you as if you were her own. But I'm so glad you are not my sister!"

"Fool!" Just hold me. They were quiet and in a while Paul dozed off but she wanted to talk, "Paul, wake up!"

"Do I have to?"

"Yes. I have an idea I want to pass by you before you get sound asleep."

"I am sound asleep."

"Now listen to me Paul. Chad wanted this land to build a housing project. Now he is going to get his chance. He can build a new village for the homeless."

"Mm," Paul moaned, "We'll talk about it honey, but for now let me sleep." His head was on her shoulder and he began to snore.

The sun was up and shinning brightly when Carol awoke to find Paul up and gone. She dressed and scurried down the stairs following the scent of fresh baked cornbread. Melba was in the kitchen stirring an extra large pan of fried grits. Just outside the door a long table held stacks of fried ham, eggs and bowls of fried grits. Fiona filled plates and yelled, "I'm out of grits!"

"Coming," Melba shouted and headed for the door with a huge pan of grits. "What else do you need out here? Need any cornbread?"

"Sacre' bleu,"Emile shook his head and laughed, "I have never seen anything like this! How can we keep up?"

The sound of hammering came from one end of the yard and Carol could see Jacob on top the rafters nailing boards and singing, "When the Saints come Marching in!"

"Where's Paul, Melba?"

"He went into town to see how things were going and to see if he still has an office. He said something about getting in touch with Chad and that he had to go to the bank."

Carol smiled, "I'll have some grits and eggs and some coffee please, right here at this table. I don't want to go outside with all that commotion. I tried to talk to Paul last night but he fell asleep. If he wants to see Chad, guess he heard everything I said. I love him so much Melba."

"Just let me finish up this pan of grits and I'll sit with you. I want to hear all you told him. I need to know what's going on." She rushed the pan of grits out to the table and returned.

Carol filled her in on McFarland's visit and the sizable check he had given her for saving his stock and race horses. "And you know what I'm going to do with part of it? I am going to ask Chad to rebuild the village!"

Melba's mouth opened and she caught her breath. "I can't believe it! He gave you that much money! Enough to do all that?"

"He sure did! Isn't it grand?"

Melba threw her arms around Carol and

kissed her. "There's not another person in this world like you child!"

"I guess you will always think of me as a child won't you Melba? But I am not a child! I am Carol, the lucky lady who inherited her grandfather's estate." She looked up at the heavens. "I know he is looking down on us and smiling. When I have finished breakfast I'm going out to talk with Jacob. I can't believe how quickly that building has gone up. We must find a way to get some heat in it. Where is Luke? I want him to drive into town and buy as many mattresses as he can find and it might not be easy because homes have been destroyed there too, but he can try." She pushed her food aside and ran outside. "Jacob," she called, "Where' is Luke?"

"Right behind you," Luke said, "What can I do for you."

"Oh Luke, good! I want you to drive into town, buy mattresses, pillows and blankets. If possible, get enough for everybody! As soon as the walls are on that building and we get some kind of heat in it, people can start sleeping in it."

"I will also need to get more supplies for the building," Luke replied. "Got to put tar paper on the roof, and a couple of windows and a door, in case we get more rain. I hope I can get everything on the truck. If I can't I'll have to make two trips."

"You do whatever you have to. Paul is in town, you can get him at his office. Do you know where that is?"

"Yes mam."

"If you need an okay on anything they can call him. And if you don't have enough room on the truck have him put things in his car. Here, let me give you a note to explain that you are picking things up for me. Some of the stores may question you."She quickly wrote a note giving him a right to charge things."As always, get all the bills, sign them and bring them to me. Now, get going!"

"Yes mam!" He smiled and headed for his truck, "Jacob," he called, "tell Mark I'll be back soon as possible! Got to do some things for Miss Carol."

She looked up at Jacob,"When do you think people will be able to sleep in here?"

"Tonight! It don't look like much Miss Carol, but to my people it will be heaven. We are making bunks for everyone. It will be crowded because we have so many. The bunks are stack bunks, as high as we can make them with little ladders to get up to each bunk. The folks will sleep on the lower bunks and the kids on the top bunks. They will love it!"

"I wish I had told Luke to get bunk size mattresses! Darn!"

"That's okay Miss Carol, he will know. We have those bunks figured out and he will know what to get. If the furniture warehouse is still standing, he'll get them!"

"Let us pray," she said. "Maybe we should put a cross on top of this building. It's going to be a home and a church for awhile."

Mark walked up behind her and said, "Good morning Miss Carol. You are up and giving orders mighty early!" He was carrying a couple of two-by-fours. "I and the men are building bunks. They won't be pretty but they will be safe. I can make a cross for you and when the reverend hears a cross is going on top, he will be shouting and hollering Hallelujah!"

"You know Mark, this building is in a very nice corner of the yard and shaded. Maybe when all this is over we can turn it into the Blue Manor Chapel. We can shingle it like the house and plant flowers around it."

"Looking ahead, Miss Carol? Does your mind ever quit?"

"It can't Mark, there is too much to be done." She laughed, "For now we will call it The Blue Manor Bunk House." She turned and left, "Got to finish my breakfast."

Mark watched her walking away and joined Jacob with, "When the Saint's go March-in in, when the saint's go march-in in, I wanna be in that number, when the Saint's go march-in in." He shook his head, "And she's gonna be in that number."

Three hours later, two trucks and a car came up the driveway. Luke got out of his truck, Kenneth got out of his and Paul got out of his car. Luke and Kenneth began to unload, tar paper, lumber, mattresses, blankets, quilts and pillows and the other men from the village came and helped.

Carol ran down to them and began asking question. "Shut up and kiss me," Paul said. "We were in luck. The warehouse was still standing and the roof was still on it. Because of the size you needed for the bunks, we were able to get the mattresses. If you had needed full size we would have been out of luck because the town's people have bought nearly all of them. The same went for the quilts and blankets, all twin size. The streets are filled with mud, some of the buildings flattened and debris everywhere. Mom will be happy to know her house is still standing and the young couple are out helping everyone clean up the streets."

Kenneth paused long enough to say, "Hi, Carol. We have more work than we had planned on, don't we?"

"We sure do! I bet you are hungry, so when you are through with all this come on in and Emile will feed you."

"Can hardly wait," Paul replied. "Now kiss me again and go away, we have work to do."

Kenneth turned away as Paul kissed her and Carol noticed. She was thankful for his help but the adoration in his eyes worried her.

Children were in the yard laughing and playing. Their clothes had been dried and they were back to normal. Emile saw to it that lunch was served to everyone. He'd made individual pies filled with meat and vegetables to go on their plates with beans and rice.

The men did not stop to eat. Most were

young enough to work, but some were crippled and old. Those sat on the porch watching the children and dozing off.

Emile feeling he should make a truly enjoyable dinner for everyone said, "Tonight I will make a sausage and chicken jambalaya. Something that can be served in individual bowls. But, Madam," he exclaimed, "in no time at all your huge refrigerator is going to be empty! I must try to make simple country foods. Melba is making pies for deserts and I am baking large cakes, much like sweet breads with bits of dried fruit and just enough sugar to make the children happy."

"Emile," Carol replied, "I know you would love to bake all your beautiful French pastries but these are hard times, sugar cookies will make them very happy. They have lived very simple lives with beans, rice, biscuits, gravy and very little meat because their families cannot afford anything else. A ham hock in a pot of beans is a treat for them. Collard greens, chard, kale, mustard greens, black-eyed pees and cornbread are a banquet to them. You can sweeten the cornbread and they will think it is dessert. I know you would love to cook all your famous delicacies, but we cannot do that. I have no idea how long we will be feeding so many. You must let the ladies help and show you the kind of food they are accustomed to. A side of salt-pork in a pot of red beans and rice with onion on top will make them very happy. And plain cakes that can feed many will be good, orange cakes, and we have lemons to make lemon frosting, make things you can slice and set on the table for them to take a piece. For now, you must stick to the simple foods. Think about what you ate when your were a child in France. Were you parents wealthy."

"Mon dieu, nous e'tions pauvres!"

"You see! You were poor and I bet you ate many potatoes."

He laughed, "Yes, we had potato soup onion soup, lentil soup, bean soup, all kinds of soups, meatloaves, pasta and stews, baked beans with honey, and broken rice because it was cheap and, as you have said, we sweetened our bread. We ate the same as these people. In my home I cook the old country way and enjoy it. I am very happy with a slice of cheese, bread and a glass of red wine. To tell the truth, my wife and children eat very simple foods. They do not expect all the delicacies I serve to the elite."

"So tonight we are having jambalaya made with pork and chicken and we will all love it," Carol said.

"Ah but madam, if I had sea food, shrimp and crab it would be even more delightful."

"I am afraid it will be awhile before we will be seeing any sea foods. However, with the river running so high the men may catch some hungry catfish and the men can go out at night and get craw-fish!"

"That would be wonderful, I can make Cajun Catfish Courtbouillon. If you have never had it, you will love it! It was not created by rich people it is made by the people who live on the bayous. That in a bowl with a piece of French bread is a wonderful meal. If they can catch allot of craw-fish we can boil them and they will love it. But with so many people, it will take too many craw-fish."

"Emile, you and Gertie are going to love one another." She looked down the drive and a very muddy Lincoln was nearing the house. "We will talk later Emile." She stepped out of the kitchen door and walked around the porch to the front and waved at Chad.

He got out of his car and made his way through the children and onto the porch, "You never stop do you my dear? I saw Paul in town; he told me your house is filled with refugees."

"That is not a nice way of putting it Chad, these are all the unfortunate people who have been flooded out of their homes and we are very happy to be able to help them. I love them all, they make me happy!

"Hum," he looked around, "if you say so! Paul told me you wanted to see me about some business. Has this storm changed your mind and now you want to sell me your land?"

"Come in and sit with me in our sunny breakfast room. It is comfortable and we will be alone. I will have Bess bring us some tea or coffee and Beingnets."

She called for Bess and she quickly returned with the coffee and the dough-nuts. He sipped his coffee and eyed her, "Well what is it to be? Are you going to sell me your land and let me build my housing project?"

"No! I want you to listen carefully and if you are not interested, I will find someone else to complete my project. As you came into the house you walked past children and mothers and were very uncomfortable with them because they look impoverished. They are and did not have much before the storm. Now, they have nothing. All their homes have been completely destroyed. Nothing was left standing in their village except their church, because it was on a hill. I can, and am willing to pay you to rebuild their homes."

He nearly choked on his doughnut and sugar went all over his lovely silk shirt. "My dear, do you have the finances to support such an undertaking?"

"I do and if you are interested, as soon as the land has dried I would like you to go there and look it over. It will need fifty homes. That is how many families are homeless. The property belongs to them and Paul and I are giving them the homes. I am not asking you to build large homes because they do not have large pieces of land. Simple two and three bedroom homes with running water and modern conveniences are all they will need." She poured herself another cup of coffee and waited. "Are you interested or should I take this to someone else?"

"And you really think you can afford this?"

"I know we can. Are you interested? If so, I will expect you to give me a reasonable price.

You will be doing something for the people. As I said, if you don't want to do it I will find someone who will."

"You have caught me by surprise. I cannot give you an immediate answer. As you stated, I should allow the area to dry out a little and then have a look at it. Perhaps one or two of the men can accompany me and show me the size of their lots. This is quite a huge undertaking my dear. But since you are so willing to be life's do-gooder and since we are related, I will have a look, draw up some plans with sketches of the homes, plus, the cost of each building. I should like to know how many children are living in each home. If it will help, I can give you sketches of homes I have built in other areas and the price of each."

"Chad," she reached over and touched his hand, "thank you. Yes, I would like to see some sketches of your rent low housing. Will they also show the interiors and what will be in them, such as sinks and bathrooms?"

"Absolutely! You definitely want fifty homes. Is that right?"

"Yes. And a little grocery store. Do you think you could do it for two million dollars?"

"If anyone else had asked me that I would have laughed right in his face. But since it is you my dear cousin, I will look at the size of the lots and decide. In all probability for that price I can build you some very nice one or two, bedroom homes, with one bath, a combination kitchen and dining room and a small living room. They will look charming and they will be safe. I can use some of the men who's homes have been destroyed and they will earn a little of your money. Knowing they are getting a free home, will give them incentive to work for a reasonable price. Now don't frown! The less the labor cost, the better the homes will be."

"I want you to start as soon as possible. This is not New York State, this is Mississippi, and things costs less in the south."

"Do not move so fast, relax. I will bring you some sketches and let you decide. First I must see the land."

"Well what are you waiting for? Get your boots on and go to it!"

The weeks and months that followed were filled with laughter, singing and prayers. Emile's family came to live at Blue Manor, and Carol was looking round and apple cheeked. This time she knew it would be a boy and his name would be James. Gertie had settled into one of the little cabins behind the house and all were happy. Carol could sit on her front porch and watch the children playing. She and Paul decided to adopt the orphans who were living with Mark.

One entire day was spent in town with the mothers and the children, buying clothing. Paul, determined to have the cottages complete with furniture and all household needs, sent in professionals to do the job. Carol and Melba, to add the finishing touch, placed a basket of bone china flowers on each table.

To complete the picture, the cottages were shingled to correspond with the mansion. Young trees were planted in each yard, lawns began to grow and low hedges on either side of the walkways led to the front steps.

Opening day arrived and Reverend Johnson and all the people, including children, walked from Blue Manor to the bridge and stopped to read the entrance sign:

"You are now entering Blue Haven."

The Reverend stood on the bridge and faced the crowd, "My people," he shouted, "the sign calls it Haven but it is Heaven. Welcome to our homes! We must thank Miss Carol and Paul for this wonderful gift."

Carol stepped forward, "Reverend, please do not give us the credit. Give it to God, because it is he who has saved you from a storm and given you all new homes. Paul and I are the tools he used. It is we who owe you our thanks for the happiness you have given us, and from this day forward when the fields are planted we will share the crops with you. Your children will be fed and clothed, as Gertie says: by the sweat of your brows."

Voices rose up in song: "God Be Just That Good! If you'd been through what we been through...You'd be thankful too! Glory – Glory Hallelujah..

Chad stood alongside Carol and Paul and smiled, "We did good," he said.

Carol turned to him in disbelief, "Yes, you did Chad and I think you did an extra special job and put your heart into it. Have you found the meaning of faith?"

He gave her a hug, "Can't be around you without believing in something! I think this is the most beautiful housing project I have ever built. It is small and has a big meaning! And because you are you, I am charging you half the price."

She through her arms around him, "You have made our grandparents proud!"

They returned to the manor and looked for Gertie, she had not been in the walk. They found her looking sad, sitting on the steps of her cabin behind the house. Alarmed, Carol asked, "Gertie, what are you doing? Why didn't you walk with us to your new home?"

"Cause ain't my home! My home gone with the storm. This my home!" She was crying.

"Yes Gertie, this is your home."

"I'is gonna be here when you gits that baby you got stickin out front you. And I'is gonna watch him grow."

A month later Gertie's prayers were answered and Carol gave birth to James.

"He gonna look like his daddy," Gertie said.

"Yes Gertie, and he's going to be a fine man like his daddy. You are going to watch him grow. He is going to be a musician, look at his fingers. I will teach him to play the piano. He will be a concert pianist."

Six months later she was apple cheeked and round again. "Paul, it's time for us to have a lawn party. The crops are nearly in and on this date three years ago we had the storm that changed all our lives. It is celebration time!"

She walked to the end of the porch and began to ring the bell and continued to ring it. All the workers in the fields looked up and came running and soon the front yard was crowded.

"What's the matter?" Luke asked.

"Nothing! I just want you all to know that tomorrow you don't work. Tomorrow we are celebrating. Three years ago we did not know if we would survive a storm. It is time now for us to remember that day with a celebration."

"My wife," Paul mumbled, "there will never be a dull moment in my life!"

"No son there will not! The only time she sits still is when she is playing the piano."

The front yard was filled with people, Emile, his wife, Bess, Fiona, Melba, Eunice and all the ladies prepared the tables. The Reverend Johnson stood on the steps of the Chapel and began to pray. "Glory!" he shouted, "We are ever blessed! Thanks be to God! Let's eat!"

As before the McFarlands and Chad with his bride to be, Rose, joined in the merriment. They would be married in the little chapel.

Kenneth sat with Paul while Eunice helped the ladies. It was a glorious night, everyone, including the children danced. Emile danced with his wife and Gertie sat on the side lines watching and clapping her hands. Now one hundred and thee years old her feet did not want to move. Carol was with child and Gertie said, "Miss Carol, "I'is tired an ole but I'is gonna be here when that chile come."

"Yes you are Gertie, and you are going to see him baptized right in our little chapel."

"When I dies," she asked, "Would you asked Reverend Johnson to say his prayers over me in the chapel? Then takes my body and puts it next to my man and my two babies."

"Yes Gertie, we will do that. But I expect you to be here at least five more years."

Gertie laughed, "Them ghosts will let you know when it my time."

"Yes Gertie, them ghosts will let me know."

"I knowed it! They's here ain't they?"

"If they are Gertie, they are good ones."

Gertie lived to see Paul junior born, and said, "I knowed he gonna be a fine man."

Chad and Rose were married in the little Chapel and a huge celebration followed. The next morning while watching everyone cleaning up, Carol asked for Gertie.

"I think she is sleeping in Miss Carol," Bess said, "celebrations are too much for her these days."

Carol went to Gertie's cabin and found her lying in bed with the patchwork comforter pulled up under her chin. "Gertie, are you all right?"

Gertie held out a gnarled wrinkled hand

and Carol held it in hers. "We's been happy Miss Carol, but my man is come for me. I see'd him standin right hind you an he smilin. He my ghost and he a good one. I'is happy to leave to goes with him."

Carol began to cry and called for Bess, "Come quickly."

"Now don't you cry Miss Carol. You is my angel. The Lord send you to me to save my family. You's done God's work. I'is happy an I'is ready to meet my maker. Can you git my boy an his chillun in here? I want's to say goodbye."

Bess ran from the room screaming and to the front porch and began to ring the bell. Luke and the workers came. He entered the cabin and knelt beside his mother. She put a shaky hand on his face. "You daddy's come for me son an I'is ready. He done wait long enough." She smiled and closed her eyes and Luke began to sob. Outside voices began to sing, "Nearer My God To Thee, Nearer To Thee..."

Carol was on her knees beside the bed when Paul and Melba entered. He put his hand on her shoulder, "We have called for Reverend Johnson and he will be here soon. Now I want you to come with me and let Gertie's family stay with her. I will see that everything is taken care of."

As was Gertie's wish, the service was held in the chapel and Reverend Johnson said his prayers over her. Her body was viewed and the casket was closed. Luke, Mark, Jacob and Paul carried her to the burial wagon and everyone walked behind singing, "Swing Low Sweet Chariot, Coming for to carry me home; Swing Low... Sweet Chariot, Coming for to Carry Me home; I looked over Jordan and what did I see...Coming for to carry me home...A band of angels a coming after me… Coming for to carry me home….

As her body was lowered into the earth the Reverend prayed:

The Lord is my shepherd; I shall not want. He maketh me to lie down in green pastures: he leadeth me beside the still waters: He restoreth my soul: he leadeth me in the paths of righteousness for his name's sake. Yea, though I walk through the valley of the shadow of death, I will fear no evil: for thou art with me; thy rod and thy staff they comfort me. Thou preparest a table before me in the presence of mine enemies: thou anointest my head with oil; my cup runneth over. Surely goodness and mercy has followed me all the days of my life and I will dwell in the house of the Lord forever.

Carol looked across at the fields beyond and touched Paul, "Do you see them?" she asked.

Paul's gaze followed hers, "Yes, Gertie, her man and her babies."

Carol lifted her hand and waved, "The house won't be the same without you," she said, "maybe you'll come and visit."

That night as they held each other Paul said, "We have just begun." Little stars danced overhead and left. "Goodnight everyone."

Made in the USA
Lexington, KY
12 May 2017